SLEEPERS, WAKE

Other Apple Paperbacks
you will enjoy:

Aliens in the Family
by Margaret Mahy

Ma and Pa Dracula
by Ann M. Martin

The Power Twins
by Ken Follet

The Secret Life of Dilly McBean
by Dorothy Haas

SLEEPERS, WAKE

Paul Samuel Jacobs

AN
APPLE
PAPERBACK

SCHOLASTIC INC.
New York Toronto London Auckland Sydney

ISBN 0-590-43299-0
ISBN 0-590-29133-5 (meets NASTA specifications)

2 3 4 5 6 7 8 9 10   00 99 98 97 96 95 94

Printed in the U.S.A.   40

To my brothers, Jerry, Eric and Howard.
They travel with me.

ONE
AWAKENING

DODY FOUND HIMSELF watching the time, measuring it by the hour, by the minute, by the second all night long. Well before first light, he had turned on his tiny bed lamp and was staring at the clock face as the digits flowed like liquid, trickle by trickle through the night in a gathering torrent of time.

He pulled out his writing pad and began a note to his friends back home, Alan and Tony. He had not seen them for years, but he still thought of them as the small boys he had left behind in California, when he and his family had sold off all their belongings and moved to the space center in Florida to wait for the launch.

Dear Alan and Tony, he wrote in a cursive of big looping letters that had not changed since he was in the fourth grade. He had learned a lot of things since he left Earth, but penmanship was not one of them.

Today is the day I told you about, when the sleepers wake. I know that I should try to sleep myself to pass the time, but I can't. I haven't been sleeping for days just thinking about what's going to happen. It will be better than a birthday, better than Halloween and Christmas, better than all the holidays I can think of. It will even be better than the day all the rockets were launched, one after another like Roman candles into the sky. I guess you must have seen that on TV, and so you know that was some day!

Today will be even better than that. After fifty years, I'm not going to have to wait anymore.

Dody said it aloud, although there was no one around who could possibly hear him.

"Fifty years!" His voice was unexpectedly high-pitched and a bit gruff, because the words were the first he had spoken for hours. It sounded like hinges that needed oiling. After fifty years, all the hinges on the spacecraft required repeated oiling, so he knew the sound of rusting hinges very well.

He went back to his writing: *My life is going to be so different after today.*

Dody could not think of anything more to say to his friends. So he signed the note in even bigger letters than he usually made so that he filled up the rest of the page. *Yours sincerely, Dody.*

He tore out the note, folded it and placed it carefully in a crumbling cardboard box that he kept under his bunk. He had filled seven such boxes with letters to Alan and Tony, because there was no way of mailing them. Someday, he hoped he would deliver all the letters. He could imagine their expressions when he handed them box after box. It would be like the excitement of picking up all the mail at the post office after a long vacation. But he wondered if he would ever see them again out here, a hundred years away from Earth by rocket. And if they met again, what would they be like? Would they be the boys he had played catch with or skipped rocks with at the pond in the city park? Or would they be old men like him, wrinkled and gray, changed so much that he would have trouble recognizing them? And if they hadn't left in the next wave of rockets, they might be gone forever, as dead as most of the things Dody had left behind.

But when he wrote to them, they lived on somehow just the way he remembered them: Tony, hitting a ball into the ivy beyond the left field fence of the Little League field, and Alan, lofting a paper airplane of his own design from the outstretched branch of their favorite live oak tree. And he was there with them, watching the ball fly over his head or throwing a plane of his own from the highest branches.

Dody looked at the digital clock and was surprised at how little it had changed. A few minutes had slipped by but the hour seemed glued into place.

"It's a very long time to be waiting," he said aloud, as if he expected a reply. After a little pause, he answered himself. "Not so long, now that it's about over."

That was the way Dody was, always jabbering away, asking questions and answering them, quarreling with himself one minute and agreeing with himself the next. A hermit behaved the same way. Like a hermit, Dody had only himself to talk to, only himself for company.

Mickey — as he called the Master In-craft Computer — finally turned on the overhead lamps in the sleeping quarters ever so faintly. The dim morning lights, which grew ever brighter, were vaguely reddish at first, like the dawn, signaling the end of another night. It was Dody's favorite time of day.

He remembered his father waking him up by placing a warm hand on his shoulder. "Don't let the sun leave you behind, little guy," his father always said in his deep, steady voice.

The glowing tubes of morning light gradually revealed the mess that was his room. An archaeologist could have written a history of Dody's life just by cataloging the clumps of clothes, the layers of equipment, the games and toys and models left in place just where Dody had finished with them. There were cartons and computer printouts and books filling up all the unused bunks. Pictures and maps and handwritten notes and drawings were pinned one on top of the other, filling every inch of wall. Miniature airplanes dangled from the ceiling — a squadron flying in tight formation. All by himself, he had managed to fill to overflowing every nook and every cranny of a room that was supposed to sleep twelve. Only his own bunk was free of debris. A little later today, he'd finally get around to tidying it all up. It was something he had been promising himself he would do for quite a few days now. Most of it he would cart down to the evacuation chamber and jettison into space, where even the junk of a lifetime would disappear in the empty vastness like so much dust.

But cleaning up could wait a little longer. He was much too excited for it now.

He got out of bed, and after kicking the floor clear to make a place for himself, he stretched as tall as he could, slowly raising his arms in the direction of the model fighter planes and bombers. As he reached up, his joints popped and his bones crackled. Then, bending his knees just a little, he dipped down low to touch his distant toes, and his whole body seemed to creak as he did so.

"That's one!" he said in a voice that was a bit less rusty now. It was a thin, reedy voice, too high-pitched to suit his body. He repeated the movements, counting aloud until he finally announced to the air, or, perhaps, to a photograph of his family that hung by itself on the wall above his bed, "That's thirty and I'm done!"

He was a little breathless. "I used to be able to do a hundred with no sweat," he explained. "Now I do just a couple and I'm winded."

He ran his hands through his stiff, gray hair, which he had long ago given up either cutting or combing. The wildness of the hair made him look a little mad, but it wasn't worth the bother to keep it neat, any more than it was to keep his room tidy.

He was dressed as usual in his uniform: gray coveralls that zipped up the front, with the red arrow insignia of the space agency over the heart. He wore his uniform day and night, remembering to change it every few days or so, but not minding much if there was a blotch of grease on a sleeve or a tear right through to a kneecap or elbow.

He wore a faded red bandana around his neck. It was quite frayed around the edges and worn through in several places. He'd begun wearing it as a boy because he thought it made him look like a cowboy, but now he wore it out of habit, hardly giving a thought to the reason. Besides, it made a handy substitute for a napkin when he was eating his dinner.

As he scuffed his way through the portal of the bedroom and into the corridor, he was still panting a little from the exercise. But, just as he did every day, he mounted his bicycle. In fact, it wasn't really a bicycle. It had three wheels and not two, a contraption he'd built for himself thirty years ago. It was close to the ground, and he rode in it feetfirst, while leaning back into a chair and pedaling forward.

With very little effort, Dody careened through the hallways of the spaceship, racing along the main corridors until he got back where he'd begun. The ship was huge, as if a thirty-story apartment building had been fitted with rockets and launched into space. There were a hundred rooms and stations and a few miles of corridors that crossed one another like intersecting boulevards. But Dody had the roads to himself as he went around and around, weaving from side to side as he pedaled, speeding up and then braking as he came dangerously close to sideswiping a wall.

When he was much younger, he'd crashed the vehicle, his body spilling out and tumbling until he was stopped by a sheet of metal. He had heard the sharp snap when the upper part of his left arm had broken. Since there was no one else to help him, he'd splinted it himself. Although it healed in time, the arm was never quite the same as the other, because it had grown together a bit shorter and a little twisted.

And forever after, the aching arm was a reminder to be careful. But it did not keep him off his bike.

Today after a short spin, he dismounted and headed straight for his favorite spot to finish his exercise. It was a wonderful room, the most splendid on the craft. The floor was a window, a broad transparent sheet, clear as glass but sturdy as steel. He called the room his solarium, the sun room, although it was decades since the sun's rays had shone into it. Dody ran and skipped and hopped in place for several minutes, looking down as he exercised at the dark vastness of space that spun by below. Of course, it was the spacecraft that was spinning and not the starry universe outside. It was the spin that created the illusion of the stars whirling by in a blur of moving lights. That was the way he saw them every morning and the way he dreamed about them at night, although he could still remember from his childhood on Earth looking up at stars that did not seem to move at all.

He dropped to his stomach to begin his daily quota of push-ups, but he paused to watch the stars, the spiraling galaxies and the stellar clouds streaking by. Stretched out, his eyes on the stars, he felt as if he were flying through the depths of space. In most of the windowless rooms and corridors of the craft, he could not sense that he was moving at almost light speed through the universe. But here he knew it because he could *feel* it.

He pushed his long body from the floor with his wiry arms. "That's one!" he said. He stopped at ten instead of his usual thirty. He'd planned to stick to the routine he had been following for fifty years, but he couldn't.

Oh, he did try a few chin-ups and some sit-ups, too, but his heart wasn't in them and hadn't been for weeks now. He pedaled himself slowly to his bedroom in the crew's quarters and headed to the bathroom. There Dody looked at his face in the mirror, noticing a faint stubble of gray hairs on his cheeks that he'd been ignoring for days. As he ran the tingling ball-shaped razor over his face until his

8

skin was smooth and shining, he tried to remember what he had looked like fifty years ago. His hair had been a light brown with a cowlick that refused to lie down; his rounded cheeks and compact nose were sprinkled with freckles from the sun. He had become faded and worn, like his bandana; he was torn and frayed like the uniform he wore.

"Look at the old guy!" he commanded his younger self. "Nothing much to look at," he answered back. "Pretty much the way you always looked."

He shed his clothes and stepped into the shower, a narrow tube that he closed about him. Its hundreds of jets sprayed him from every angle, first with soap and then with clear, hot water, and finally with warm air to dry him. It still reminded him of a car wash.

Sometimes he went for weeks without a shower. After all, why did it matter? There was no one to see him, no one to smell him, no one to care whether he was pigpen dirty or car-wash clean. Mickey the computer didn't care.

But today, of all days, it did matter. Dody remembered for once to pick up his old coveralls and drop them into the laundry, along with a mound of discarded clothes he had neglected for a couple of months. Then he pulled a bright new uniform from the clean clothes bin, one without any holes in it, one that was as stiff and neatly creased as it had been when it was new. Dody didn't much like the feel of it against his skin, but he wore it anyway because of the special occasion.

After tying his old bandana around his neck, he

ambled over to the dining hall, his limbs feeling a little looser now that he had exercised and taken a warm shower. He found himself singing as he walked. His own voice calmed and comforted him. Loudly he sang, "My country 'tis of thee, sweet land of liberty, of thee I sing." His twangy voice seemed to fill the entire ship when he got to the part: "From every mountainside, let freedom ring."

Where was his country? he wondered. The one he had left behind he would likely never live to see again, as much as he wanted to. And he had no idea what the land ahead of him might be like. It was light-years distant from Earth, a colony that travelers from the first wave of rockets should have reached and settled thirty years before. He felt like one of the European settlers who followed Columbus and Magellan and Vasco da Gama to make a home of their own in a faraway land.

The dining hall, one of several on the ship, could seat twelve at a time, but as he had for the past five decades, Dody ate breakfast alone. He typed the necessary code into the computer terminal to tell Mickey he was ready to eat.

It was Wednesday, so he had pancakes for breakfast as he had for the past 2,600-odd Wednesdays. Mickey was programmed that way: French toast on Monday, Tuesday eggs and bacon, Wednesday pancakes with a choice of synthetic maple or blueberry syrup. Dody was tired of pancakes on Wednesdays, even with a choice of syrup, and just as tired of eggs and bacon on Tuesdays. He was tired of the unending succession of lonely, predictable breakfasts. But when he tried to change the routine, Mickey had flatly refused to allow it, just as he refused to allow changing wake-up times or adding extra portions of dessert.

"That's outside your jurisdiction, Dody," Mickey would say, in what was supposed to be a calming voice, showing neither anger nor excitement. Dody knew that Mickey was just a collection of circuit boards and wires, with no feelings to express, with a voice designed to be pleasant and polite. But Dody imagined that Mickey sounded disapproving, the way his father or mother would if he'd been caught doing something he shouldn't. The voice irritated him and once he'd even tried to turn it off completely by reprogramming the computer, but Mickey had objected, saying simply, "That's outside your jurisdiction, Dody."

That had been years ago. But in all that time, he had not stopped trying to convince an unbending Mickey to alter the way the ship was run.

Nevertheless, because it was Wednesday, the oven popped open with the usual stack of pancakes, and Dody pushed aside the plates that had collected from several previous meals and ate what he could. He thought about clearing away the dishes, and maybe if there had been other people around to notice what a mess the dining hall was in, he would have. Instead, he decided to clean up a little later, after he played

11

a game of chess with Mickey, so that the time would pass a little more quickly.

Sitting at a computer terminal in his bedroom, Dody soon grew impatient with the game and chose to take advantage of a weakness in Mickey's programming that he had first discovered fifteen years before. Although he knew he would beat Mickey, Dody still felt disappointed that he had.

"Dumb computer brain!" Dody said to an unhearing Mickey, as soon as he was able to type "checkmate" into the terminal. "You're such a lousy chess player, I don't know why I bother to play you anymore."

Mickey wasn't insulted. "That is checkmate," the computer affirmed, as he always did when he lost a chess game. "Congratulations, Dody. You played a fine game. Would you like to play another?" Mickey spoke so cheerfully that it took away what little pleasure there might have been in beating him.

Dody typed an emphatic *NO!* and walked over to the music room. Long ago, Dody had read all of the books in the craft's library more than once — even the two encyclopedias. He had listened to all the ship's music many times over, watched all of the movies, completed and repeated all of the tutorials, and endlessly played all of the games in Mickey's catalog of programs.

Dody was bored with all of it. But he did not curse the designers of the spacecraft, because they had thought to do one thing that saved him from years of boredom and probably madness, too. They had put a pipe organ on board, and they had filled the music room's shelves with the finest of music. In a lifetime, Dody could not have mastered it all, even though he played for hours every day. He had begun playing the music of Bach when he was a boy learning the piano back on Earth, hating the lessons and the long hours of practice. His mother had told him he had to do it.

At first, it was a memory of his mother's voice that started him playing again. "Trust me, Dody," she had said. "If you work hard at your lessons now, you'll be glad you did when you're older."

Now, a man of almost sixty, he sat down at the bench in front of the keyboard and lost himself in the music that had been written centuries before. He tossed his head back and forth and swayed to the rhythms of melody and counterpoint, humming along with the main parts while his feet danced over the pedal keys. Dody, after all the years of practice, had become very, very good, even though there was no one to appreciate his playing.

Time moved quickly for a change as the music devoured the remainder of the morning.

The last piece he played was one of his favorites, a hymn by Bach called, "Sleepers, Wake!" He'd first learned the melody when he was a boy, and he'd never tired of it. It was melancholy music, recalling his family's living room at home with a spinet off in the corner under a drawing in bright pastels. His mother had sat beside him, playing the left hand while he played the right. She'd smelled of lavender perfume, and a faint ghost of the scent seemed to fill the room every time he played the ship's pipe organ.

He stopped suddenly and looked at his watch. "Oh, gee," he said. "I don't want to be late." He forgot all about cleaning up his room or clearing the dishes.

In a panic, he dashed into a corridor that led to a room deep within the body of the craft. Above the entranceway, he saw a metallic plaque, engraved with the words *Hibernetics One*. He touched the sign and rubbed it for good luck, leaving a smudge of fingerprints. Then he typed his code into the locking mechanism. The portal moved aside with a cricketlike chirrup. The chamber was lit like a photographic darkroom, aglow in a dim, red light. Arranged in berths about him, stacked six high on every wall, were coffinlike boxes, made of gleaming steel, each with a handle on its side. At the head of each box was a transparent bubble, through which Dody could make out the profile of a face. On one wall, however, the box on the second shelf from the top was different; there was no face inside its globe of clear plastic, only a black emptiness.

"This one hatched a long time ago," Dody said, tapping the empty globe.

Years before Dody often came to this room just to look at the faces, to study them and to remember.

But as he grew older, the memories proved too painful, and he visited less and less often. "Jeeminee, I haven't been in this room for seven years," he said a bit guiltily. "There wasn't anything I could've done. I tried everything I could think of, but there wasn't anything."

The faces within the clear bubbles did not hear him, or at least did not show it if they did. Instead, they slept on and on, as they had for the past fifty years, their red eyelids closed, their red faces still as death.

But suddenly a panel of instruments that hung from the ceiling came alive with flashing lights. "Twelve noon relative time. Preparing to inject chambers 1A through 1D," a speaker announced in a voice that was distinctly Mickey's.

Dody's heart began to pound and quiver within his chest, like a sizable frog trying to hop up into his throat.

Behind him, suddenly and without warning, came a prolonged hiss from one bank of boxes. "What's that?" he asked. He could see that four of the transparent bubbles were filling with a dense vapor that obscured the faces. The singing sound of the gas jets stopped, and the room was so silent for a moment or two that Dody could hear the rapid beating of his own heart.

"Twelve oh nine, relative time. Evacuating chambers 1A through 1D," Mickey announced. Dody could hear the churning of a motor and then the whoosh of vacuum pulling the foggy gas away from the faces. He studied them closely now that he could see them plainly again. Their ruddy faces belonged to a man and a woman far younger than Dody and to a boy and a girl. The noses of the children were alike — short and turned up a little at the end — the plump cheeks, too, and so was the wide placement of the eyes. The woman and the two children were dusted with freckles, but the man was not.

Dody knew he would only have to wait a few minutes now. He began to dance with impatience, hopping about like a jaybird in a neighborhood full of cats. "Twelve thirteen, relative time. Decompression and full oxygenation," Mickey declared.

"Oh, frabjous day!" Dody shouted. "Callooh! Callay!"

"Twelve fourteen, relative time. Sensors show blood gases within normal limits. Body temperature at thirty-seven degrees Celsius. Chambers unlocked," said Mickey, in his usual, matter-of-fact way.

Dody rushed up to the wall, ducking down to glance first at the man's face, then the woman's, then the boy's and then the girl's. He bobbed up and down, looking for even the smallest sign of life: a twitch, a blink, an open eye. And then he saw that the woman yawned, swallowed and smacked her lips together. And the side of her box fell open as she turned the handle from within and then stretched out her limbs.

The freckles had been preserved on her face, visible through a rosy tan; her light-brown hair was still bleached golden from the sun.

"I'm so very dry," she said hoarsely to no one in particular, her eyes not yet open. "I want a drink of water."

To Dody, there was no more beautiful sound on earth than that raspy whisper of a voice. It was even more lovely than Bach on the pipe organ, more exhilarating than the most lilting soprano. He moved so close to her that he could feel her warm breath upon his face. He could smell the chemicals, sharp and stinging. Her eyes blinked open.

"Father!" she exclaimed. "Oh, Papa," she said, throwing her arms around Dody's head. And then her voice seemed troubled as she pushed him away. "But you're not supposed to be here, Father. We left you behind. Is something the matter?"

"I'm not your father," Dody said very softly. She blinked a few more times as if to clear her vision.

"No, I can see you're not," the woman said, her forehead furrowed as she tried to remember. "But you look so much like him."

"I guess I do," Dody said. She did not seem to recognize him at all. "He and I are related, too."

She rose from her berth and stood shakily under the red lamps, staring at him with great intensity.

The woman looked as if she were trying to think of a word or name that was on the tip of her tongue.

"Who are you?" the woman demanded at last. "I have to know who you are."

"I'm Dody," he whispered. "David Mark Ramsey."

"Dody?" she said in disbelief, reaching out to touch the faded, ragged red bandana. "You aren't my little Dody!" But then she examined him again, and her eyes opened very, very wide. "Dody," she said, crushing him to her. "What's happened to you, my little baby boy?"

TWO
SECOND SUN

BEFORE DODY COULD EXPLAIN what had happened, the other sleepers started to stir. First there was the man in the bottom berth. He stretched his cramped legs through the open side of his box, and then followed with a pair of arms, a head and then the rest of his torso, rather like a lizard emerging from an egg. He sat for a moment on the floor, his hands on the ground for support. The man's hair was thick and curly, his body compact and muscular. His skin was rough and red, as if he'd spent the past few days gardening or playing on the beach under a bright sun.

Sprawled out on the floor, he looked like a soccer player who had collided with a goalpost — a dazed athlete, not yet ready to leap up and resume the game. Warily his eyes moved up the tall figure of Dody, who was helping his mother stay on her feet.

Despite his bent head and careless slouch, at several inches above six feet, Dody towered over her. When the younger man's gaze finally came to rest on Dody's face, he seemed even more alarmed than Dody's mother had been. "Where did you come from?" he cried out.

"I've been here the whole time," Dody began. "I just woke up a little earlier than the rest of you. That's all."

"You don't recognize him, Sam?" Dody's mother asked, reaching out an arm to help the man stand up.

"He does look faintly familiar. A little like your father, Betsy. Oh, now wait a minute here. Your father didn't manage to stow away on board with us, did he?"

Betsy Ramsey began to cry. "Father's dead by now," she said. "Mother, too."

"We knew they would be, Betsy," the man said gently. "Long before we started out, we knew there would be no turning back. They're all dead by now, most everyone we knew. It's been a long time, Lady Liz. There's a whole new generation back on Earth."

A whole new generation, Dody thought. Generations, if his calculations were right. But what about Tony and Alan? His two best friends in the world, in the universe. By now they should be sleepers, too, on their own journey through space. But there was no time to think about Tony and Alan, not just now.

"You still haven't told me who the old man is,"

the man said, jabbing a thumb in Dody's direction.

Before anyone could answer, the boy in the top-most of the berths jumped to the ground. He must have been about thirteen, and like the others, he wore the gray space agency coveralls with the red insignia. He looked at his watch and gave a little yelp. "Asleep for one hundred and seven years." He yawned. "I wonder why I still feel so sleepy. And, boy, am I ready for a whopping breakfast. Where are the eats?" Then he noticed Dody. "Who's the old guy, Mom?"

Dody's mother tried to speak, but broke into sobs again.

Suddenly they all heard a muffled shout from the second berth. "Get me out of here! I'm stuck!" Dody quickly grabbed a handle on the remaining unopened box and twisted it, allowing the side to fall open the way the others had. "Grandpa?" asked a girl as she awkwardly emerged from her berth. She was eleven and tall for her age, long-limbed and almost pretty, Dody thought.

"That guy can't be Gramps, can he?" asked the boy.

"No, he's not Grandpa," said Dody's mother.

"Where's Dody gone to?" asked the boy. "He isn't . . . he isn't dead, is he?"

"He can't be *dead*," the girl said with surprising certainty. "He just isn't awake yet."

Dody was afraid to speak. He had looked forward to this moment for fifty years. He had plotted it and planned it, hundreds — no thousands — of times. But nothing was going as he had imagined it would. He had wanted his father to take him in his arms and rough up his hair the way he'd always done after they'd been separated for a while. Back then, he would have worried that someone might see him like that, locked in his father's grip so tight that he couldn't breathe. Now, Dody wanted to be hugged and held, no matter who could see, even Tony and Alan, even the entire fourth-grade class at Oliver Wendell Holmes Elementary.

Dody had expected his mother to cry over him and cuddle him and comfort him, but instead she seemed in shock, and he, too, felt numb — and disappointed. Through those many lonely years, he had never fully considered what the climax of all his waiting would be. In his mind, the moment was going to be an eruption of infinite happiness, like a solar flare reaching up and out from the surface of the faraway sun. Reality could never shine so brightly. Painfully and patiently, he had waited for this reunion, worried the whole time that something might go wrong, that one of them might have entered that sleep from which there is no waking or that he himself might die before seeing them again. But their hibernation had been without the slightest flaw. They had slept for a hundred seven years and woken up, unchanged.

He had awakened fifty years before the others — fifty years too soon. He had survived — old and wheezy, his left arm crooked and shorter than the other from that long-ago break — but still very much alive.

Now he saw that his family — his father, his mother, his brother, Bobby, and his sister, Elaine — were not elated but confused. To them, the entire hundred seven years of their hibernation seemed no longer than a night's uninterrupted sleep. That was the way the scientists and engineers had planned it. They would awaken refreshed and otherwise unchanged, ready to find and explore the planets of distant stars, to help the first wave of space travelers who had left Earth so many years before them.

But for Dody the last fifty years had been spent in longing and in solitude. And, now, instead of the embraces of happy reunion he had expected, he was greeted only by puzzlement and questions. His mother alone had come close to behaving as he had expected. It was like the worst possible nightmare of childhood. It was as if he had been away and was never missed, and then was unrecognized on his return.

"Where's Dody, Dad?" Bobby repeated.

It was at that moment that Dody's father, Samuel Clemens Ramsey, the captain of the spacecraft *Wanderer*, first recognized the old man standing before him.

"Is it you?" he asked, jumping to his feet. "Oh, fella," he blubbered, before he pulled the old man into his arms and ran his hands through that wild, gray thatch of hair. "How's my little man?" he said.

Dody could not find his voice.

"Well, you've grown," said his father, who had suddenly become calmer. The captain had always been like that, able to right himself quickly from any emotional upheaval. It was the reason he had been chosen for his job. He could ignore his feelings and behave correctly in a crisis. And yet now his voice was gravelly, and each word seemed to have to struggle to escape from his throat. "You're quite the man now, I can see."

"I don't look the same, I know," Dody said. His family could not possibly be ready for how much he had changed. He was almost two feet taller than when they all first went to sleep. He was even taller than his father now and his father was a tall man. "But inside I'm still mostly the same. I'm still *me*."

No longer groggy, his mother was the first to understand fully what had happened.

"Has it been," she faltered, "*terribly* lonely?"

Dody cried at last, just as he'd known he would. "Terribly," he said, blowing his nose into his red bandana. It was the first time he had cried in almost fifty years. The last time was in those first few days when he'd found himself alone, the only one on the ship to be wakened from the chemical sleep that was meant to pass the time of their long space journey. No one could ever know just how lonely it had been, waiting all those years for the sleepers to wake.

In that time, Dody had grown up in some ways, but not in others. Yes, he had learned a great deal. He'd studied and read a lot — a book a day until he had exhausted the ship's library. He'd mastered mathematics and physics, biology and chemistry. He'd read all of Dickens and most of Melville. But he'd never done the things that he had once expected to do by the time he'd grown old. He'd never been off to college, never found a job and moved into an apartment, never vacationed in Yellowstone or traveled to England, never found a wife and had children of his own. He'd never even been to junior high. And with no one to talk to but a computer, he was still very much a boy — an odd sort of boy with an old man's body and a mind full of facts that no nine-year-old could possibly have learned. Yet the soul of him, the self that sits behind the eyes and looks out at and judges the world outside, was still a boy's soul, no matter how old the body and no matter how learned the mind.

"Who's the old guy?" Bobby asked again, but now showing his impatience by stamping a foot against the bare metal floor.

Elaine suddenly knew the answer. "Oh, *now* I know who you are," she said. She ran up to Dody, threw her arms around his neck, lifted her legs off the ground and hung there, the way she would have from the limb of a tree. She was so much smaller than Dody now, so light that he swung her around and around.

"El, I missed you maybe most of all," Dody said.

"You mean he's *Dody*?" Bobby said, finally catching on. "It's like Rip Van Winkle!"

"Except he's the one who was awake and we were the ones who kept on sleeping," Elaine explained, still clinging to her younger — or was he older? — brother.

Just then the full force of what had happened hit Bobby. He knew now that the little boy that he'd expected to find when they all woke up from their deepest of sleep was no more. He began to cry, without even trying to hide it. That was such a rare and unexpected occurrence that it made Elaine cry as well. Soon they were all crying, even their father.

And there followed a commotion of shrieking and embracing, of laughing and applauding, of speeches and exclamations, of kisses and tears, just as if a great war had ended and world peace had been proclaimed.

It was without a doubt the happiest and saddest moment of Dody's life, all at once, and he wished that time could be suspended like a snapshot and that they could all linger in the moment, frozen forever.

But the hubbub died at last, and Bobby remembered how hungry he had just been. "Any food left aboard?" he asked.

"Oh," Dody said, "I forgot how hungry you guys must be. There's lots of food in the dining room."

"The mess, you mean," corrected the captain,

who was a navy man before he became a space traveler.

How did he know? Dody wondered, now wishing he'd gotten around to cleaning up all those dishes.

"I should check the charts and inspect my craft," said the captain. "Then we can start waking up the others."

There were weeks of hard work ahead, Dody knew. The crew would be awakened in clusters, no more than five or six at a time until all three hundred were revived. The *Wanderer* would soon be as alive and busy as a small village. Betsy and Sam Ramsey would have little time for their children, who would have important tasks of their own to perform. The hollow calm of the ship would be forever ended.

"That can wait, Sam, until we've had some food," Betsy Ramsey said. She glanced at Dody. "This will be quite a feast for all of us."

"A Thanksgiving Day feast," Dody said. "And Christmas dinner. And Easter supper."

And so it was that the Ramseys walked down the empty corridors with Dody in the middle, their arms locked together for comfort and courage, on their way to a midday meal.

"Will Dody always have to be so different?" Elaine asked as they reached the dining hall. "So old, I mean."

No matter what he hoped, Dody knew the answer. "There's no turning back the clock," he said.

"Poor Dody," said Elaine, who burrowed her face into her brother's chest.

"Let's not talk of it anymore," their mother said, tears in her eyes again. "What's important is that we're all well and all here together."

She stopped crying when she noticed the condition of the galley. "This *is* a mess, Dody," she said. "I'm surprised at you. I thought you were old enough to clean up after yourself!" She began to slip plates into the washer.

"He's plenty old enough," Bobby said.

Ignoring him, Dody went to the computer terminal to order up a meal for five — the same chicken à *la* king that was always served for lunch on Wednesdays. But never had it tasted quite as good as it did that day.

As they chewed the rehydrated chicken, Dody found himself doing a lot of talking and not much eating, mostly because his mother wouldn't let him do both at the same time.

"For the first few days, I kept busy exploring the ship. You know, I'd never really seen it all before. I didn't even know where the sleeping quarters were, and when I found ours I realized I didn't know the code I needed to open the portal. I slept the first two nights underneath this table."

Elaine ducked her head down and slapped her hand against the thinly carpeted floor. "That would make for a hard night's sleep," she said.

"I didn't even know how to order up a meal,"

Dody said to his sister. "For the first two days all I had to eat were the candy bars I'd stuffed into my pockets before we took off." Just then, Bobby reached deep into his coveralls and pulled out a collection of assorted sweets that he had pocketed more than a century before.

"You did that, too?" Dody asked.

"I was the one who told you to do it. Don't you remember?"

Bobby unwrapped a candy bar.

"I bet Dody would like one," the captain said.

Dody nodded. "I haven't had a candy bar for a long time."

"Fifty years," said Elaine.

"I sure could use one," Dody said in the same tone of voice he might have used to ask for a drink of water while close to dying of thirst in a desert.

"Bobby'll be glad to share them," the captain said. "Won't you, son?"

"I guess so," Bobby replied, without meaning it.

But to Dody's amazement, Bobby handed him one of his candy bars, the kind filled with nuts and caramel and covered in light chocolate. Back home Bobby would never have given up quite so easily.

"You remembered my favorite kind," Dody said.

"Sure, I remember," said Bobby.

"Like it was yesterday," Elaine said.

Dody tore through the familiar wrapper and continued talking as he chomped on the candy bar, which was as fresh as the day they had blasted into space, although it had a faint chemical smell.

"I thought I was going to starve to death," Dody said, continuing his story.

"Just like Robinson Crusoe," Bobby said. "Marooned and alone. You had to learn to survive by yourself." For Bobby nothing could have been better than to have such a great adventure and he envied Dody the chance.

"It's not like Robinson Crusoe at all," Elaine said. "There was no shipwreck, for one thing."

"Thank goodness," said their mother. "Do go on with your story, Dody."

"I began to fool around on the computer terminal, and I figured out that Mickey could teach me how to operate almost everything on board."

"User friendly," said the captain, in self-congratulation. "We worked with the programmers so that even a kid could figure it out."

"I'd never call Mickey *friendly*," Dody said. "He's always seemed kind of *mean* to me. But he did teach me how to take care of myself on board and kept after me until I had all of the answers right on my schoolwork."

"Schoolwork?" Bobby said in disbelief. "While the rest of us were asleep you've been doing schoolwork?"

"Yes, we programmed it in so you kids could keep up," the captain said.

"Dody, you always did like school so much more than your brother," Dody's mother said, approvingly.

"I like school, too," Elaine reminded them.

"I had a lot of time on my hands," Dody apologized to Bobby. "And I kept hoping I'd figure out how to wake you guys up. But I never could."

"Why did Dody wake up and not any of the others?" his mother asked.

"Maybe he's a light sleeper," Bobby said.

"I tracked down the problem a long time ago," Dody explained. "It was a little error in my program."

"Human error," the captain said. "Like packing a parachute, sooner or later you'd expect a mistake. It was bound to happen at some time or another with five thousand ships taking off all at once, each with a crew of three hundred."

It had been a wonderful sight, Dody thought. Thousands of rockets leaving the earth, all within a few hours, each one riding across the sky on a hot cone of flame that was brighter than the brightest shooting star. It was the second wave of rockets that came thirty years after the first. If everything worked as it should, they would find established colonies on many of the planets, and the seeds of humankind would grow and flourish outside the solar system.

Dody had been able to watch most of the rocket firings, one after the other from the huge launchpad, until an hour before it was the *Wanderer*'s turn. He couldn't remember the takeoff because he was already asleep by then along with most of the crew. He recalled going into hibernation. The smell of the gases was as sharp and sweet as the witch hazel his

31

grandfather used after shaving. He had felt the numbness spread down the nose and throat into the lungs and the heart and then out to his limbs so that his whole body tingled before he fell asleep.

It had been strangely pleasant, the opposite of what he'd felt when he woke up and found himself all alone.

"I wish you would've got one of us up," Dody's mother said. Dody could tell she was on the verge of crying again.

"I tried," Dody said quietly. "I tried to change the program, but Mickey — the computer, I mean — wouldn't let me."

"That would have been outside his jurisdiction, Betsy," said the captain. "There was nothing he could do. It was a necessary security measure. Only a few of us on board have the authority to override the master computer program." He rubbed his eyes. "I'm sorry, son."

"I did learn how to chart our course and plot destination," Dody said, unable to keep from bragging.

"I'm surprised you had clearance for that," the captain said. "But I'm proud you were able to teach yourself navigation."

"And I learned how to get inside the control room."

"That is definitely outside your jurisdiction," the captain said. He sounded troubled.

"And in just a few days we'll be ready for landing," Dody said.

"Impossible," said the captain. "We're still six months away from our destination."

"I speeded up the craft just a little," Dody said.

"Damnation!" said the captain.

"We're right on course, following the beacon."

"Then there *is* a signal." The captain was pleased. They were following the trail blazed by a ship from the first launch years before. Those older ships weren't altogether reliable. Some had exploded at takeoff. Others could be expected to fail along the way. But their beacon ship had survived the journey. The captain looked as if he were about to reach over and pat Dody on the head. "That means the first ship got this far at least."

"Got here and found a place to land safely," Dody said. "I can show you on the telescopic screen in the control room."

He bounded up and was out the portal without even putting his candy bar wrapper in the disposal.

By the time his family caught up with him, he had turned on the projector. The room was arranged like a small theater, with two dozen chairs facing a screen that filled an entire wall. All the surfaces of the room were curved and padded, the walls textured like eggshells and painted white.

In the center of the screen, in the midst of thousands — millions — of stars, was one a hundred times brighter than any of the others, an orange-red sphere that glowed warmly among so many cool and distant lights.

Dody sat in a chair in the front row and began

changing the lenses, until the star was magnified many times over, until it became a giant red sun that filled most of the screen.

"Look at our second sun," said Betsy Ramsey.

"Do you mean Dody or the star?" Elaine asked.

"You can see the planets," Dody said without paying Elaine the slightest attention. "Eleven of them. This is the one with the beacon."

He pointed to a dark round shape silhouetted against the burning sphere of the sun. "It has to have life on it. It's got all the signs. The spectrograph shows water, an atmosphere of nitrogen and oxygen and an average temperature of twenty-nine degrees Celsius."

"It's better than we could have hoped," said his father, genuinely impressed. "You've done very well. But there is no way we'll be ready for a landing very soon. Not if we're concerned about safety. There's just too much to do. We'll have to start terminating hibernation for the rest of the crew. That could take weeks. And we'll want a few weeks more to make adjustments for the new destination. We could speed things up, but I don't see any reason for the hurry."

Dody wanted to argue. He had been waiting so long for so many things, the thought of waiting even a day more to reach the planet he had found in the loneliness of space seemed unbearable.

He could already imagine a landing on the fifth planet from this, their second sun. They would find settlers there, he was sure, the heroes who had taken off from Earth in the first wave of rockets a generation before the Ramseys had. There would be a thriving colony by now, a new home for the *Wanderer*'s crew and a whole new planet to explore.

There would be oceans there and beaches. Dody thought of setting off in search of a sandy shore and of stretching out on the beach as the waves rolled in and the sunlight warmed his pale skin. His whole family would be there, Elaine and Bobby and his parents setting up a giant umbrella to give shade to their blanket. There would be fried chicken and potato chips and fresh tomatoes and sweet soda in bottles still wet from an icy cooler. Real food, Dody thought. And his father and mother and sister and big brother would throw him into the waves, and they would ride before the swells on inner tubes, stopping only when they scraped against the sand, the white foam surging past them.

For the first time in fifty years, he was part of a family again. He was disappointed that he'd have to wait for the landing, but he had found a new contentment. It lifted his fluttering heart just to know that his father and mother would take care of him again. They were in charge now. It was their job, and no longer his own, to be sure they all got to their destination.

"Yes," he said aloud, forgetting that he was no longer alone, "I want to play on the beach the way we used to."

"Are you all right?" his mother asked.

35

He was old, as old as his grandfather, bent and creaking, and there was no changing that, no reversing time. But here with this family, he could still be the youngest child again, the little boy.

"I'm fine, just fine," said Dody, with a comfortable sigh. He would have to write a letter to Tony and Alan.

THREE
LAND HO!

DODY SNEEZED. It was not a particularly violent sneeze, not one that would startle an innocent passerby or cause a policeman to draw a gun. It wasn't a messy sneeze, either, not the kind that required unfurling an oversized white handkerchief to manage. Just an ordinary, little, stifled sneeze. But for Dody it might have been a geyser, an earthquake, a volcanic eruption. It had been fifty years since the last time he had so much as sniffled, and this average — you might even say puny — little sneeze startled him.

"*Gesundheit!*" Bobby said.

"God bless you," said a more delicate Elaine.

Dody had forgotten whether or not the polite response to either exclamation should be "Thank you," but before he could say anything he sneezed again. His head felt heavy, as if silt were collecting behind his eyes.

Dody and his family were on another inspection tour of the spacecraft, their fourth in the past week. During that whole time, Captain Ramsey had been unable to awaken any of the other crew members and he wanted to know what had happened. They had walked the miles of corridors. They had inspected the galleys and the computer stations. They had cataloged the damp corners of mold and of rust, the broken fans and leaking valves. They found nothing extraordinary after a century. There was more wear than might have been expected from just one person's being awake for only part of that time. But there was no damage that would have an effect on the central computer or the sleeping chambers it controlled.

They had found nothing that explained why the sleepers refused to awaken.

In the red glow of Hibernetics Two, Dody studied sleeping faces he had not seen for decades.

He and Elaine and Bobby had played softball with Billy Madsen just a week before the launch. Even in his long sleep the boy's hair looked as if it had been tossed by a recent wind. He was an older boy, closer to Bobby's age than Dody's, but Dody remembered Billy as being particularly kind, telling him to push his hands together and move them up the handle of the bat if he wanted to get a hit. Billy didn't need to choke up at all. He had a loose, easy swing that could power a ball out of the infield anywhere he wanted to hit it.

And above Billy slept his sister, Anna. Even as she lay there, her mouth was open, almost in a smile. Dody saw the small space between her front teeth that she might have been able to whistle through. How Dody had loved that little gap and the sweet young face of the girl, who was just nine or ten and unchanged in all these years.

Dody untied his bandana and buried his face in it.

"You *do* seem to have a cold," his mother said.

But Elaine knew better. "It's not just a cold," she said. "He's crying."

"Why would he be crying?" the captain asked. "The crew is doing well. Once we figure out how to wake them, they'll all be just fine." He wanted to sound confident and always did, whatever misgivings he might have had. "No need to cry, for gosh sakes."

Dody took a deep breath and tried to stop. "It's just a cold, Dad," he said.

"And where could he have caught a cold?" his father asked his mother, who was a doctor, one of three on board the *Wanderer*.

"We must have brought the virus along with us," she said. "But I think there's something wrong besides a cold, isn't there, Dody?"

How could he explain it to them? Dody wondered. It was suddenly seeing Billy and Anna after all these years, seeing that they were just the same as they'd been the day of the launch. Just as Elaine and Bobby and his parents were the same. Time had stopped in its tracks for them. It had waited for them patiently while they slept. Sure, he was worried for them, worried that they might stay asleep forever, as good as dead, like wax models stretched out in their coffinlike berths.

That was not why he was crying. His father would somehow find a way to wake them. And when he did, Billy and Anna would continue their life just where time had left them. And that was what grieved Dody. Carried by time as the others slept, he had left them behind. Left them as far behind as Earth — light-years away.

Even if there were softball games on the planet they were speeding toward, even if there were parks and beaches to play on, even if they all landed safely and started a new life there together, they would always be somewhere behind him.

As much as he wanted to play with them, as much as they permitted him to, he would always be a distance ahead, an orphan of time.

"Oh, Dody, my poor Dody," said his mother, placing an arm around him. "I wish we could make you all better."

"It's just a cold," he said, sniffling. "Just a cold."

They returned to the *Wanderer*'s control room, the largest room on board the ship, except for the huge launching bays that held the landing craft. Under a curved ceiling, there were two dozen adjustable seats that could be pushed back like reclining chairs. The room had its own toilets and snack station, so that a crew could work around the clock if necessary to prepare for a landing or make a course correction.

The large viewing screen flickered to life when the captain depressed a square red button on the control panel. At the moment he did so, a nearby button turned to green. The screen filled with stars, brilliant lights set against a blackness that was perfect and deep. More clicks of square buttons, and the image changed in flashes until Dody's father found what he was looking for, the circle of pale green and tan that was the fifth planet from their second sun. Thin wisps of clouds spiraled over it. In the center was a great blue sea. All along its shores, Dody thought, there must be beaches where ocean waves flung themselves forever against a gentle slope of sand.

The lights of the control panel began flashing green and red in sequence, like blinking bulbs on a Christmas tree. Dody helped his father work the controls, the two of them moving furiously, while buzzers blared and beepers sounded. Dody was surprised to find he was more skillful at operating the ship than his father. He was quicker and more certain of what needed to be done.

On the other hand, Bobby and Elaine seemed to be constantly getting in the way. When it came to running the ship, they were totally useless, Dody

41

soon discovered. Finally Captain Ramsey said to them, quite curtly, "You two! Take a seat at the back or you'll have to go to your rooms."

Bobby paused long enough to consider whether or not to argue. He might have said, "That's not fair. Why does Dody get to work the controls when we can't?" Or he might have said, "We didn't do anything, Dad!" Maybe it was the look on their father's face, the eyes narrow and the jaw muscles tight, but neither Bobby nor Elaine said a word.

The two of them minded better than Dody, who did not listen very well to what his parents told him. He was the one who was out of practice when it came to paying attention. Over the past week, since the others woke up, he was always forgetting to put things away and then balking when his parents reminded him. He had no use for the daily chores assigned to each of the three Ramsey children.

He saw no reason at all, for example, to make up his bed every morning as the lights glowed red with the dawn. "Do I have to?" he would whine, whenever his mother reminded him.

"Ship's rules," Betsy Ramsey would say. "You know that."

"He's such a baby!" Elaine had said. "He acts like he's nine."

Dody would flush with embarrassment. Probably she was right. He didn't mean to be forgetful or difficult, but the habits of decades seemed impossible to change. A lot of the time, he still *felt* like a kid, even if his hair was gray and his face creased and wrinkled. *He* hadn't changed as much as his appearance had. He was still the same Dody — couldn't they see that? They had no right to expect him to behave like a grown-up.

But at other times, he knew he had changed and wanted the others to recognize it.

The lights on the control panel stopped flashing, and the noisy alarms were quiet at last. "Mission accomplished, high orbit achieved," Mickey announced over all the ship's speakers.

For the first time since he was a child, Dody realized he had arrived somewhere. He was no longer in between places while speeding through space enroute to a distant star. He and his father had parked the spaceship 98,000 miles above planet 5. At last there was an above and a below to the universe, an up and a down, a solid here instead of an imagined there.

They had stopped in a position so distant from their own sun that light itself would have to travel for years to reach them. If they could pick the sun out of the billions of stars all around them, it would have seemed just a little pinprick of light. And, of course, the earth was invisible, as if it had been swallowed up after they'd left it behind. Their home in California and the tree Dody loved to climb and the beach where they hunted for rounded bits of colored glass were unimaginably far away. But it was comforting to know that he might soon have solid ground beneath him again, a planet with gravity and sunshine and room to roam. And perhaps even beaches. Sandy beaches.

"Your computer friend has finally done something right, Dody," said Captain Ramsey. There was a ragged, impatient edge to his voice that reminded Dody of times back on Earth when his father was displeased with him. "For once, he's done something without a hitch."

"You can't really blame Mickey for the programming mistakes, Dad," Dody said.

"Mickey's done very well, considering," chimed in Dody's mother.

Over the past week, they had discovered dozens of computer errors. Some were only minor: For years, Mickey had sometimes tossed the ship's dishes into open space, rather than reusing them.

"Maybe he doesn't like to wash dishes," Elaine had said.

But other mistakes were much more serious. Some of the programs made no allowance for the extra day added in leap years, and as a result, certain parts of Mickey's brain lagged almost a month behind the rest. It took the captain several days to reset all the computer's clocks so that distances and destinations could be calculated without confusion. For two days, while Dody and the captain checked through his memory, Mickey was like a patient recovering from brain surgery. He lost his voice and could only speak by spelling out his words, letter by letter, on the computer screen.

Dody and his father were both convinced now that it was probably a programming error that kept the other crew members from waking up, just like the mistake that had awakened Dody too soon.

The *Wanderer*'s chief computer expert could certainly solve the problem, but that was Billy Madsen's father and he was still asleep in Hibernetics Two.

Without a crew, they might as well turn around and head for Earth.

Captain Ramsey tried one more time to wake the others, following each step of the routine that Mickey displayed on the control room's computer screen, but again he failed to wake them.

"They aren't dead. The ship hasn't been damaged. I should be able to wake them!" the captain said. For the first time, he seemed worried and that troubled Dody.

His father and mother were supposed to rescue him and make everything right. The beacon had been calling them here, and now they were supposed to land and find the colony that had come before and finish the job of exploring and settling the planet. Other waves of colonists from Earth would follow, passing their long journey in hibernation and only turning back to Earth if no beacons had been left for them to follow. But most likely, the new immigrants from Earth would join a thriving community that had set down its roots on a distant world.

Now Dody was not so certain that any of it would ever happen according to plan. He was impatient and even angry with his father, who he noticed was not especially good with computers.

Dody sneezed again.

The captain pushed his chair back into a reclining position and started it revolving slowly as he gazed up at the bowed ceiling. "There has to be a way to fix the program, even if we have to take the whole system down and reprogram it from scratch."

"You still think it's a glitch?" asked Betsy Ramsey.

Dody was distracted by the sound of the word, and he began saying it aloud, almost singing it in that curiously high-pitched voice of his. "A glitch, a glitch, a glitch, a glitch," he said. It was one of those words that sound ridiculous when it was repeated over and over. "A glitch, a glitch, a glitch," Dody sang.

"Please, Dody, I'm trying to think," the captain said.

Dody reddened. He had been trying very hard to stop talking out loud to himself with his family around.

"He talks to himself a lot," said Bobby, still angry that Dody sat at the control panel while he could not. "I guess that's what happens when you've got nobody else to talk to for so long."

"Dody?" asked Elaine. "When you talk to yourself, do you ever get into arguments?"

"Sometimes," Dody admitted.

"And who wins?" she said, delighted with the thought. "You or yourself?"

Dody sneezed again.

"Stop picking on Dody," Betsy Ramsey said. In the past week, she often had stepped in to shield the last born of her children from the onslaughts of the other two. Dody was pleased that she did. He had been a long time without a mother to protect him. "You feel a little feverish, I think," she said, putting her cool hand on his forehead and then stroking his hair.

Dody remembered how he was treated when he'd had colds back on Earth. He'd stay home from school, and his mother or father would fix him a hot cup of weak tea, with sugar and a slice of lemon. He'd been a sickly little boy, and there had been concern over whether he could withstand the long trip — even talk that he should be left behind with his grandparents. "Allergies," his mother had said. "There's no ragweed or mulberry pollen in space. He'll be fine."

And she'd been right. Except for the broken arm, he'd been healthy all the time, until his cold.

He sneezed again.

"Maybe you ought to go to bed, Dody," his mother said.

The captain turned to his wife and raised an eyebrow, as if he were about to say something. Before he could speak, Bobby and Elaine said it for him. " 'Don't baby him, Betsy,' " they said at the same time and then laughed.

The captain had been repeating that to her for days now.

"It's true," the captain said. "You do baby him,

Betsy. And look at him. Does he look like a baby to you?"

For a moment all the Ramseys stared at Dody who was looking up at the image of planet 5 and had stopped paying attention to his family. They noticed the droop of his eyes, the wattle of skin under his chin and the tufts of long hairs that shot up from his dark eyebrows. Whatever other feelings they might have had about Dody, their faces all displayed a single emotion: They were saddened by the sight of him, grieved by the loss of the little boy he had been.

"He'll always be my little boy," Dody's mother said softly. "Always."

Luckily Dody wasn't paying them much attention. He had taken out his pad and was busily writing Tony and Alan, his pencil noisily scratching out each word.

You can't believe the planet we are heading for. It has huge blue seas and a strange green mass crisscrossing it like the letter X. The green X looks like it's clinging to the planet like a starfish on a rock. If Dad can get the crew awake, we'll land there soon, right in the middle of the X where the four arms come together. That's where the beacon is. It's where the first ship must have landed. I can hardly wait to see them. I wonder if they made it through all right and what they found down there. Maybe someday, you can meet me there. By then I'll know my way around the place. Very truly yours, Dody.

Dody ripped out the page, creased it tightly and

jammed it into a pocket. The flapping and crinkling of paper seemed a tumult in the mournful quiet of the room.

Dody turned to his father. "Why do we have to wait?" he asked. "Why can't we go down there by ourselves?" he asked. "I know how to fly the lander. I could fly it all by myself if you let me. And maybe some of the crew down there can help us wake up everybody else."

"I've thought of taking the lander down," the captain said, "but it's too dangerous. We don't know what we'll find down there."

"But the beacon's working. That must mean that the first ship made it through all right."

"All it means is that the beacon's working."

"But, Dad . . ."

The captain began punching the buttons on the control panel again, going through the sequence that was supposed to wake up the rest of his crew one more time. He hit the keys instead of tapping them, as if the force of the blows would help to rouse the others from their sleep.

Dody remembered now that his father was usually cool in a crisis, but could also be impatient and even short-tempered if he was not moving ahead toward his goal. On a hike through the woods back home, with a full eighty-pound pack on his back, he would charge ahead of the others, walking in long strides that left Dody in his dust. Only Bobby even attempted to keep up with him.

Dody thought about the thousands of ships that had headed off from Earth, each to its own destination, to thousands of stars that might have planets, which might be suitable for human life. He wondered if all the ships had computer problems like the one that had awakened him early or the one that now made it impossible to wake the rest of the crew.

"That's why there are so many ships," Dody concluded aloud. "A lot of them won't complete their missions safely."

Dody's remark was the plain truth, but Captain Ramsey considered it treason. "My job is to make sure that my craft is one of those that gets where it's going and gets us all there in one piece. And nobody'd better say that we're not going to make it." He glared at Dody as if he were not a child of his at all, but a stranger, an outsider with no claim to tolerance or sympathy.

"Maybe," said Betsy Ramsey hastily, "it would be a good time for you children to leave your father and me alone for a while."

Bobby and Elaine needed no more direct order than that. They moved quickly for the control room portal. Dody rose to join them.

"Not you," the captain said sharply. "I might need your help."

"Let him go with the other two," Dody's mother pleaded. "The three of them could use some time together."

Sam Ramsey softened. "I suppose there's no real

hurry," he said. "I expect the three of you to find something to do that won't get you into trouble."

Dody was annoyed to be treated just like one of the other children. "Come on," he said to Bobby and Elaine. "I'll show you parts of this ship that you've never seen. I know every inch of the place."

The two followed after him.

"I'll take you to one of the launching bays," Dody offered, once the portal clanked shut behind them.

"Dad said they were off limits," Bobby reminded him.

"Oh, come on," said an exasperated Elaine. "Whenever we want to do something *fun*, Bobby, you're always saying, 'Dad said this,' or 'Dad said that.' Dody's a grown-up person. If we go with him, I'm sure it's all right."

"We're not going to hurt anything," Dody argued. "I just want you to get a good look at a lander."

"Well, I guess there's no harm in just looking," Bobby said.

If he had been blindfolded and spun around several times, Dody could still have found his way to one of the launching bays. There were four of them, each with its own lander.

The *Wanderer* was like all the spaceships in the second star fleet. The living quarters and working stations on each ship were arranged in a column around a hollow core many stories high. The gigantic cluster of engines was in the very center, held in place by metal struts, like so many shiny spokes connecting it to a spinning wheel. The spin was important. After years of manned spaceflight, the space agency had learned that weightlessness was harmful to space travelers on long journeys. Spinning the ship had the effect of throwing its contents to the gently curving outer walls, creating an artificial gravity. As a result, the inhabitants could walk normally inside the spaceship, their feet against the outer hull. Because of the curve, Dody always felt he was walking uphill. His calf muscles bulged from the exercise.

The ship's security system should have prevented all but a few of the crew from entering the launching bays alone. However, Dody had long ago figured out the code he needed to punch into the lock, and he was happy to show Bobby and Elaine how easily he could make the large inner doors of the bay swing open.

"I had to bypass Mickey's security to get access to the launching bays," Dody bragged. It was one of a very few triumphs over Mickey.

"Wowie!" Bobby yelled, as he got his first glimpse of the landing vehicle. It was two stories high, a sweeping wedge of polished metal that looked as if it had been coated with silver. Dody beamed. He'd finally done something that impressed his big brother.

Bobby ran directly for the lander, but as he reached up to touch its shining surface, Dody screamed.

"Don't touch it!" he said, just in time to stop

Bobby in his tracks barely out of reach of the lander.

Bobby turned around. "Why not?" he asked. "I wasn't going to hurt anything."

"The oil on your fingers," Dody said. "It'll ruin the polish. And your sweat could etch the metal."

"So?"

"The rough spots might burn up in the atmosphere," Dody said.

"So?"

"The entire lander could go up in flames, like a cinder flying out of a fireplace."

"Oh." Bobby pulled back his hand quickly as if he had scorched it.

"You've got to put on gloves," Dody said, his face twisting as he tried to avoid another sneeze.

"Show me where I can find some," Bobby said, all eagerness again.

"I thought you just wanted to take a look," Elaine reminded him.

"I want to get a look *inside*," Bobby said.

"I don't know whether we should," Elaine said.

"We're not going to touch anything," Dody said. "I've been inside a lot of times."

"I guess there's no harm in just looking," she said.

The three Ramseys walked just below the lander, to a spot on the floor that was marked off with yellow lines and stripes like a traffic island on a highway. In the middle of this area, attached to a pipe, was a small computer terminal into which Dody typed a message to Mickey. With a great whirring of engines, a square section of metal was slowly lowered from the landing craft's winglike form. The elevator device stopped soundlessly in front of them. The Ramsey children stepped onto the lowered platform and, at the press of a button, were lifted into the craft itself.

The inside of the lander was as cramped as the spaceship was spacious. There was room for twelve crew members, six in the forward compartment or control room, and six more in the aft, all crammed tightly together like pencils in a box. The walls and ceiling and floors were padded and the chairs were contoured to protect the crew during sudden take-offs and jolting landings.

"Where do they keep the food?" Bobby asked.

"And where's the toilet?" Elaine said.

"Maybe we shouldn't be here," Dody said.

"We just got here!" Bobby said with contempt. "You're older and bigger than me, and you're still just like a little kid."

That shut Dody up. He wasn't a kid, and he was tired of being treated like one. He could show Bobby just how grown up he could be if he wanted to.

"I'm in a hurry, Dody," Elaine said.

"You're right," he said to the two of them. "We won't hurt anything." He showed his sister where to find the toilet.

"And you're probably in a hurry, too," Dody said to Bobby. "With the right computer code, you won't have to starve." He fingered a special code into the snack station, which dispensed three squeeze bottles of a pink liquid and three tubes that looked like they should have been filled with toothpaste.

Dody and Bobby settled back into two chairs in the forward compartment.

Dody was half miserable now. He was sure that his father would be furious with the three of them if he knew where they'd gone. His cold was getting worse, he could feel it. His throat was raw and scratchy, his nose had begun to run, his eyes felt as if they were bulging from his head.

But there was another part of Dody that was enjoying himself. He loved showing Bobby how easy it was to squirt the pink liquid into the mouth. And the tart drink made his throat feel a little better.

"Snack time?" Elaine asked when she rejoined her brothers. Bobby replied by tossing a squeeze bottle and a toothpaste tube in her general direction. To Dody's surprise, she pulled them out of the air expertly, one after the other. He had forgotten that she was the most athletic one in the family. She was a good swimmer and an even better baseball player.

"Not bad, huh?" Elaine said as she pulled off the lid of the bottle and began sucking out its contents. "Punch," she said, pleased, and then squeezed a tan dollop from the tube. She nibbled at it. "It's like peanut butter only it's cashews," she said. "What a great treat, Dody. Thanks."

"Any candy bars stashed away?" asked Bobby, who was not as pleased with the snack.

"Let me show you something else," Dody said. He began pushing a sequence of buttons on the control panel. Suddenly a screen opened up in the ceiling above them. On it was a projection of planet 5, most of its giant X visible now, without a cloud to obscure it, like a pale green hand clutching the planet.

"That's a neat trick," Bobby said, rising to his feet and standing next to Dody, alongside the instrument panel. "Now what does this button do?"

"Push it and find out," Dody said.

When Bobby did, the button next to it changed from red to green — from NO GO to GO.

"Push that one, too," Dody said.

Bobby obeyed, pushing a whole sequence of buttons that changed in turn from red to green — from NO GO to GO — until the entire panel was glowing green.

And then there was a deep rumble, like the roll of a bass drum or the peal of distant thunder. Dody smiled as Bobby's jaw dropped open. The lander gave off a low whining sound, as if it were answering the rumbling call that had come before.

"Now, you've done it, Bobby!" Elaine screamed. She was as angry as she was frightened. "You're always doing things without thinking!"

"That's not true!" said Bobby. "I don't *always* do anything."

From hidden speakers came Mickey's cool and unmistakable voice. "Prepare for launch," the computer said with the same calm that he would have used to ask them to get ready for lunch.

"Dody, do something!" Elaine pleaded.

Dody knew what he needed to do to stop the

engines from firing. There was still time if he wanted to, but the next few seconds were critical.

"Ten seconds to launch," said an indifferent Mickey.

"You don't really know how to fly this thing?" Bobby asked.

"Sure, I do," Dody said. "It's a piece of cake."

"Six . . . five," said Mickey.

"We'll be in big trouble with Dad," Elaine said.

"Four . . . three," said Mickey.

Even then Dody might have stopped the launch. All he needed to do was press two of the control panel buttons at the same time. It took two hands and a long reach. It was simple.

But Dody was not sure he wanted to stop. If his father wasn't ready to begin to explore the planet, then maybe the three of them would do it on their own.

He wasn't sure what to do, and it didn't help that his head was heavy or that his ears buzzed from his cold. But he lost all chance of stopping them when he began the deepest, loudest and most powerful sneeze in the whole of his long life.

"Gesundheit!" said Bobby.

"God bless," said Elaine.

"Launch underway," said Mickey.

And all three of the Ramseys were thrown back into their chairs as the sleek-skinned lander shot through the bay's open outer doors and headed for planet 5.

FOUR
THE LANDING PARTY

"IT'S ALL HIS FAULT," Bobby said.

"Why is it *his* fault?" Elaine demanded. "You pushed the buttons."

"He's right, you know," Dody said. "It was my idea." He'd wanted to show them how much he knew. And instead he'd shown that he could be as reckless as a small boy.

Elaine felt too sick to be angry. They were weightless in the landing craft as they hurtled toward planet 5. She was feeling as green as she would on a roller coaster or a bobbing boat at sea. Bobby, on the other hand, was celebrating the freedom from gravity by turning somersaults in midair.

"You can turn us around," Elaine said.

"I don't know how," said Dody, who sat at the control panel turning through an operations manual that would have taken him a week to read.

"But you said you could land us," Elaine said.

"It's all automatic, once we're launched," Dody said. "Mickey finds the beacon and flies us down. Anyone could land us on automatic. Getting back, I'm not so sure about."

Elaine was too queasy to protest. Instead, she sat as still as she could, twisting a curl of hair that hung in front of an ear. It made her sick just to watch Bobby, who cavorted and tumbled through the air, so she tried not to look at him. Her face was as colorless and puffy as bread dough. Even her freckles had faded.

"Tell us about time again, Dody," she asked gently.

Dody riffled the pages of the manual. There was a way to turn off the automatic pilot and take control of the lander if he had the right computer code. But Mickey, who still thought of Dody as nine years old, would never let him do it.

If Captain Ramsey had been on board, he, of course, could have changed course or even ordered the lander to return to its bay on the *Wanderer*. So could any of a dozen adult crew members with the authority to override Mickey. But none of the Ramsey children, including Dody, had the power to do so.

At first after their unexpected launch, Dody was sure that their father would find a way to call them back to the *Wanderer*. But they had not heard from Captain Ramsey at all. Maybe there was another glitch in Mickey's program, Dody thought, or maybe some crucial piece of equipment had failed.

Whatever the problem, they were racing ahead toward an alien and perhaps hostile world, driven by a computer that had already made too many mistakes and could certainly make many more. Would they land softly as they were supposed to, Dody wondered, or would their craft slam into the surface of the planet like a bullet?

Dody had tried hard not to say anything that would frighten his brother and sister, which wasn't easy because he'd become accustomed to thinking aloud. All the while his silent, inner voice was talking to his parents. "Oh, please rescue us," it said. "Mom. Dad. Please."

He blew his nose loudly into the bandana that he'd taken from his neck, and then he wadded the rag up and stuffed it into one of his pockets in his coveralls.

The viewing screen was filled with the strange geography of planet 5. Through thin, swirling clouds, Dody could make out a blue sea in the middle of what appeared to be a desert of reddish sand. The great green arms of the giant X that hugged the globe turned more fully into view. They seemed to by trying to squeeze the life out of the planet, Dody thought.

He tried one last time to convince Mickey to change course and send them back to the spaceship *Wanderer*. But Mickey reminded him: "Landing craft course correction is outside your jurisdiction, Dody."

Perhaps it was Dody's imagination, but Mickey sounded as if he were a little sad to have to say it, as if he felt sorry for them, but that there was nothing he could do. When Dody continued to type program changes into the computer terminal, however, Mickey changed his tune, warning ominously, "If you persist in trying to tamper with the landing program, Dody, I will have no choice but to terminate all communication."

Angrily Dody depressed the *z* on the keyboard and held it down until the computer screen filled with *z*'s before turning dark.

"Is Mickey getting in a few *z*'s?" Bobby asked. He gave an exaggerated yawn as he settled down into his chair again. "Well, I'm pretty sleepy myself."

"Please, Dody," Elaine said. Her face was white now, as white as flour, as white as clown makeup, as white as a refrigerator door. "There's nothing else you can do. Please tell us about time."

The youngest of the three Ramseys — or oldest, depending on your point of view — ran his hand through his long, gray hair. Maybe Elaine was right, Dody thought. It might be best to pass the time in idle conversation rather than worry about events he could not control.

"Time," he said, sniffling as he wondered where he ought to begin. "There are all sorts of time."

"I know," said Bobby. "There's snack time, lunchtime and dinnertime, not to mention breakfast time, suppertime and high tea."

"You can't be hungry again!" said Elaine. The

thought of food made her feel even queasier.

"What time is it back home, Dody?" asked Bobby, who was suddenly more serious.

"Three thousand years or so after launch," he said after calculating the numbers on his fingers. "About 5000 A.D., Earth time, I would guess," Dody said. "I could get Mickey to give us a more exact date, but I'm tired of talking to him."

"Isn't that real time?" Elaine asked. "If we never left home, wouldn't we be living in 5000 A.D.?"

"In 5000 A.D. we'd be deader than doornails," Bobby said.

"I'm not sure I know what's real time." Dody leaned back in his reclining chair. They'd given him a chance to show how much he knew, and he would have to show them that he knew quite a lot. "When you rush through space at nearly the speed of light, time for you is very different from what it is on Earth. Einstein figured that out. And then Hoffman finally calculated it out more exactly. The clocks on Earth are turning much faster than the clocks on board this ship. The clocks we have with us record the way we feel time on the *Wanderer*, not what we'd feel if we stayed on Earth."

"Where time flies," Bobby interjected.

"Time seems slower when we're moving away from Earth this fast," Dody said. "Aboard the *Wanderer*, our atomic clocks show the passage of one hundred seven years; on Earth, the same sort of clocks would show three thousand or so."

"Still, I don't look a day older than when I left," Elaine said.

"That's because you've been protected from time. You've been in a biological deep freeze," Dody said a bit sadly.

"Like a frozen mackerel," Bobby observed. "But you got unfrozen, Dody. That's why you're so different now."

"I'm not so different," Dody said.

"Sure you are. You're bigger. And hairier. And droopier. Even if you still do act like a little kid a lot of the time."

"I do not," Dody said, remembering now how angry he used to get at Bobby when he picked on him.

"Tell us about Hoffman," said Elaine, changing the subject. "You know everything there is to know about him. Tell us about him, Dody. Please."

"He's the greatest genius of his age," said Dody. "Greater than even Einstein." He loved to talk about Hoffman. "Hoffman," he repeated as if the very name was musical. His cold was forgotten. He'd even forgotten, for a moment, where the landing craft was heading.

"He must've been a dreadful man," Elaine said.

"What do you mean *dreadful?*" Dody was puzzled. "Just because he discovered the truth about the sun?"

"The Hoffman factor," Elaine yawned. Just as she had expected, the talk had begun to relax her. "Isn't it true that if it wasn't for the Hoffman factor, we wouldn't be here at all?"

"What is the Hoffman factor, anyway?" Bobby asked. "I knew all about it once, but I kind of forgot."

"It's a fact about the universe, not dreadful or nice, just true," Dody said. "Hoffman was the first to measure the effect of gravity on time. And he figured out that the sun would survive only a few million years more, not billions more like most scientists expected."

" 'The fact that launched a thousand ships,' " Elaine recited from a poem that every school kid was supposed to know. "A horrible man."

"But don't you see, he's a hero." Dody had read all the books about Hoffman, and he knew all the lessons by heart. "Hoffman's calculations showed that the sun and Earth are doomed, but in making them, he may have saved humankind. He's the reason we're out here searching for a new home. If we succeed, people will be able to outlast the sun and colonize the universe."

"Hip, hip, hoorah," Bobby said, without much enthusiasm.

"Even a million years is lots of time," said Elaine. "Why would anyone care what was going to happen in a million years, when a couple of thousand years is just about as much as anybody can imagine?"

"Hoffman said that we'd probably never get another chance to get away from the solar system," Dody said. "Civilizations come and go."

"Like the Egyptians," said Elaine.

"Exactly," said Dody. "Nobody knows for sure how they built the pyramids. It's all forgotten now. Maybe people will forget how to build rockets. Then we'd be stuck on Earth when the sun explodes and everybody burns to a crisp."

"Like french fries," Bobby said. "Still I wish we'd waited a couple hundred thousand years to do the exploring, because I'd rather be home playing baseball."

"So would I," Elaine admitted.

"Not me," Dody said.

"You never could hit a baseball," Bobby pointed out.

"This is one of humanity's greatest adventures," protested Dody. "It's historical."

"Don't you ever want to eat a chocolate bar again?" Bobby asked.

"Or go on a hike in a forest?" Elaine added.

"Or eat barbecued chicken?"

"Or visit the South Seas?"

"Or roast a marshmallow?"

"Or ski down a mountain?"

"Or munch on popcorn?"

"I hate Hoffman," said Elaine.

"So do I," Bobby agreed.

Dody felt defeated. As his brother and sister knew, he was never very good at arguing. But he knew they were wrong. He knew that there was no better place in the universe to be than here, racing toward a distant planet where humans might settle a new world and keep their kind alive.

He remembered the day their parents first told the three of them about their journey. Elaine had cried because they couldn't take along Cleopatra, her tabby cat. And Bobby was angry that he would miss the next baseball season. Dody wasn't entirely happy with leaving his home behind, either, but he was thrilled by the thought of rocketing into space and exploring distant worlds. Who knew what might await them!

"Where's this guy Hoffman now?" Bobby asked. "Safe at home, I bet!"

"Thoroughly dead by this time," said Elaine.

"He's not dead at all," Dody said. "He was the first to volunteer for the mission. He left Earth in the first wave of rockets, the one that left before we were born." Dody paused before revealing the best news of all and the reason that he was in such a hurry to land on planet 5.

"We're following his beacon," Dody said. "Hoffman's right down there, where the X crosses."

"I wish we'd stayed home," said Elaine. "I want to go back."

"It wouldn't be the same there," Dody said.

Tony and Alan had left long ago. Most everything else had withered and decayed. The oak tree behind their house would be gone. The house, too. His grandparents. Dody wondered what had happened in all the years since they had left. Whether the earth had heated up as some predicted. Whether an ice age had settled in. What wars had been fought? What revolutions? With their journey nearing its end, they were as far away from their own time as they had once been from the Greeks who had sailed away to fight the Trojan War. Nothing could stay the same for that long.

Dody blew his nose into his bandana.

Mickey, who automatically came to life whenever there was an important announcement to make, interrupted them. "Preparations underway for entry and descent," he announced. "All systems go."

"To Hoffman!" Dody said, trying to sound brave about it.

"To Hoffman," said Bobby.

"To a smooth and gentle landing," said Elaine.

The next half hour passed very quickly, as if time had speeded up for them. Planet 5 was so close now that they could only see a part of it on the viewing screen as they rocketed around it, moving from night to day to night again.

They looked for lights as they circled the planet, but saw none, or any other earthly signs of civilization.

The instruments told them that there was life here and there, most densely along the arms of the giant X that covered thousands of miles of the globe's surface. But if Hoffman and his crew had survived, Dody wondered, wouldn't there be lights or a radio message to greet them, instead of just the beacon?

"What if we run into alien creatures down there?" Bobby asked. "What do we say to them?"

" 'Take me to your leader' is the usual thing to say." Elaine laughed. The color had returned to her cheeks.

"Come on, be serious," Bobby said. "We ought to be ready for this."

"There could be intelligent beings on some of the planets," Dody agreed. "Besides the colonists from Earth."

"And stupid beings, too," Bobby said. "What if we run into their version of a cow, say, or a cat? It's going to seem pretty dumb if we try talking to a horse."

"Maybe their horses here are just as smart as we are," Elaine said. "Smarter even."

"I wonder if we are going to need guns," Bobby asked. "There could be beasts and vicious monsters."

"Or worse, crooks and criminals," Elaine said.

"More likely green plants," Dody said. "I just hope they're edible."

"I hate greens," said Bobby.

"I just hope they don't want to eat us," Elaine said.

Mickey interrupted them again. "Prepare for landing," he said rather urgently, Dody thought.

Automatically their chairs folded back into landing position, the arms enfolding them protectively.

"I wish we didn't have to do this," Elaine said.

"I wish we land safely," Dody said.

"I wish I went to the bathroom when I had the chance," said Bobby.

The landing craft began to shake as it buffeted through the atmosphere. As the craft slowed, they could hear the roar of its rockets resisting gravity and lowering them to the landing spot, where the arms of the giant X crossed on planet 5.

Was it Dody's imagination, or did he hear what sounded like a long, loud scream from outside the craft as its hot rocket fire touched the surface of this world so very far from their own? The shrieking stopped as the vehicle dropped with a final thump.

The craft rested at a slight angle, as if it had landed on a sizable object. The tilt made it hard to get out of their chairs.

"Are you two OK?" Dody asked.

"I'm all right," Elaine said, as if she might be feeling queasy again and wasn't really sure.

"That was fun," Bobby said. "Better than a roller coaster."

But Dody, who never liked roller coasters, was wet with sweat.

"Let's get out of here and explore," Bobby said, bounding up from his chair and struggling up the little walkway to the landing craft's hatch area.

"Mickey won't let us," Dody said. He'd taken out the operations manual to see what to do next. "Not until we've been on the ground long enough for him to run all the tests. There's the atmosphere to consider. It might not be good enough for breathing.

We might need to carry oxygen to avoid contaminated air."

But Bobby began to type a message into a keyboard mounted on a beam near the hatchway.

"You're just wasting your time," Dody said impatiently. "Mickey won't let you out until he's ready." But to Dody's astonishment, and perhaps Bobby's, too, the floor that Bobby stood on began to drop. He was being lowered by the elevator mechanism and carried out of the landing craft.

"Stop it!" Dody cried, before he had time to consider that Bobby did not know how to stop it even if he'd wanted to.

Bobby was out of sight before Dody managed to get out of his own chair.

Just then, a sweet warm breeze, a zephyr filled with the scent of wildflowers and pine, swept into the craft. Dody's nostrils quivered.

For years, Dody had only known the smell of the spaceship, of the musty recycled atmosphere that hadn't been replenished with fresh air for more than a century. He had grown used to the faintly fetid smell. But the sudden breeze was a feast to his nose, a mix of air so thickly fragrant that it left him almost tipsy. It cleared his passageways. His head felt light again. In an instant, he was cured of his cold.

Dody loved the smell. It reminded him of a hike through a forest in the Sierra Nevada, over a trail of decaying pine needles. And for a moment he was transported, by his nose, back in time. He'd gathered small pinecones, on the way to a mountain lake.

Halfway up the trail they'd frozen at the sight of a bear, who eyed their backpacks as if he knew they were stuffed with food as well as camping gear. Dody's father had scooped up rocks and thrown them at the animal. One stone had hit the animal's side with a thump.

The bear swung around and ran up the trail ahead of them.

His father knew how to handle emergencies, Dody thought. And now he was overwhelmed with the wish that his father could be with them.

Wishes wouldn't help Bobby, if he was in trouble.

With Elaine close behind him, Dody raced to the hatchway and retrieved the exit platform. Bobby had disappeared; he must have walked out onto the surface of the unknown planet or else evaporated into its atmosphere.

"The air must be all right," Dody said. "We don't seem to be dead."

"How can you be sure?" Elaine asked.

"It's balmy here," Dody said, ignoring her and remembering a word he had not used in more than a century. "Balmy," he repeated, liking the musical sound of it.

"Maybe too balmy," his sister said nervously. "I wouldn't want to be embalmed here. Let's find Bobby."

Dody punched a code into the computer terminal,

and Mickey announced: "The atmosphere of planet 5 is suitable for respiration."

"Big surprise," Elaine said.

"Let's go look for Bobby," said Dody. But when he instructed the computer to lower them to the planet surface, Mickey refused. "That operation is outside your jurisdiction, Dody."

"Let me try," Elaine said, "I'm older than you." And, perhaps because of her age, Mickey obeyed her instructions and lowered them to the ground.

Outside, the brilliance of this, their second sun, was blinding. Dody had to struggle to keep his eyes open. He wanted to look around at the landscape, but the light was just too bright. He hadn't felt the warmth of the sun since he was a little boy. He had an urge to take off his shirt and bask in it. He began a little dance, or a shuffling that might be taken for a dance. The ground felt spongy beneath his feet. He started to sing an all-but-forgotten song. "You are my sunshine," he sang, only a little off-key, "my only sunshine."

"Stop it, Dody," Elaine ordered. "I don't see Bobby anywhere!" And then she gasped. "We're not alone."

Dody blinked in the direction in which she pointed. His eyes were gradually adjusting to the glare. She was right. Off in the distance, several hundred feet away, was a cluster of what Dody made out to be people. Or at least they appeared to have the right general shape to be humans.

"Who are they?" Dody said aloud.

"I don't think they're munchkins," Elaine replied.

Whoever they were — and now Dody could make out that there were dozens of them — they were walking — no, running — straight toward Dody and Elaine.

FIVE
A CHILDREN'S ARMY

THEY WERE RUNNING TOGETHER, a pack of them, their feet hitting the ground in perfect synchrony, first twenty-four right feet, then twenty-four left. All dressed in gray, one behind the other, they seemed like a single creature — a giant caterpillar or a centipede. The orderly motion frightened Dody. These people moved like an army, he thought.

What terrified him most was the quiet. Their feet struck with a steady rhythm on the spongy earth, but the sound was muted like a heartbeat, more felt than heard. And not one of the running figures cried out to the newcomers who had emerged from the landing craft, either to greet them or to warn them of a coming battle. It was like watching a movie with the sound turned off, except that the missing noise rang loud in Dody's imaginings.

He wanted to turn around and run back to the

lander, where he and Elaine could have barricaded themselves in while trying to persuade Mickey to start up the engines and let them take off again. The craft was only a short distance away. But Bobby was outside somewhere, and they couldn't leave him behind. As the crowd of runners came closer with each step, Dody saw that they wore the same space agency coveralls that everyone on board the *Wanderer* wore. They looked like space travelers who had come from Earth in the first migration. That should have been reassuring, but it wasn't.

He noticed something else as the runners moved closer and closer: These were not full-sized people at all. They were children, most of them smaller than his sister, Elaine.

"Well, maybe they *are* munchkins," Elaine said with some relief.

But to Dody, tall as he was, they seemed huge. Several looked bigger and older than he would have been if he had not awakened before he was supposed to. They were about the size of the big kids who bullied him on the school playground — as big as the blond boy back home who had bloodied his nose once. And there were so many of them! Dody's legs felt frozen.

He looked for Bobby, hoping that his brother would rescue them. There wasn't a trace of him to be seen. By squinting as he scanned the horizon, Dody could see that the craft had landed on a vast, almost featureless plain. There were no trees and no noticeable boulders or even rocks, just faintly green ground. The surface was smooth except for crusty places here and there — lime-peel-colored scars and scabs raised up slightly on ground that was otherwise as smooth as a baby's skin. A pale green baby, the color of the inside of a ripe avocado. There was no obvious place for Bobby to hide except for a few dark round spots that might be holes in the ground or entrances to burrows.

And there was no sign of a spaceship or lander from the first wave of travelers who had headed here so many years before. Where was the beacon that had called them to this very spot? Dody wondered.

As he looked around, he noticed that the lander rested on a cup of land with a puckered edge. The craft sat unevenly in this crater, tilting to one side even more than when they had left it.

Dody and Elaine found themselves backing up a little as the army of running children advanced. For all the energy of their movement — their legs were churning like pistons on a locomotive — the runners were making rather slow progress. The children seemed to be clutching swords, but the weapons did not gleam as real ones might be expected to in the bright daylight. Toy swords for a children's army, Dody thought. But even that didn't comfort him.

The runners drew their swords as they approached and began waving the weapons above their heads the way Saracens might have swirled their scimitars around and around to frighten off the Crusaders or the way Visigoths might have charged the Roman legions. Dody began moving backward in earnest at the curious sight of a horde of children acting like barbarians on a rampage, but he stopped when he saw that Elaine stood her ground.

"What do we do now?" Dody asked. "I vote we run for it."

"Don't act like such a baby," Elaine said. "They're just a bunch of kids."

Dody knew she was right, but he still felt uneasy.

"Hi, kids!" Elaine shouted in a voice as loud as a police siren.

The words had an unaccountable effect on the charging children, for all at once they stopped. "Hi, kids," Elaine repeated, in a more normal voice. There was no need to shout. The frozen forms were nearer to her than the length of a bowling lane. If she'd had a ball, she might have knocked them down like so many pins.

One boy stepped forward from the group. He was slightly taller than the rest, a little taller than Elaine, but still more than a head shorter than Dody. His hair was so thick and curly that he might have been a Ramsey cousin. He had skin that was almost paper-white. Maybe that was what seemed so strange about these children. They should all have been lobster-red or brown as walnut shells from playing in the intense sunlight of planet 5. There wasn't a tan or a freckle among them.

The boy was smiling. His white teeth, which were

as straight and evenly spaced as any orthodontist could have made them, gleamed in the midday light. "Aren't you afraid of us?" he asked, running the sounds together so that it sounded like a single word: "arnchafraidovus."

"You speak English!" Dody almost shouted.

"What did you think we'd speak?" the boy said. But the way he said it could have been spelled "wadjathinkweedspeak."

It should have been comforting to hear his own language spoken much the way it was back home in California. But Dody was still ill at ease.

"I never thought about it," Dody said, and the tall boy and all the other children began to laugh.

"That's a funny one," said a girl with golden hair. "The big girl spoke to us in English and now you're surprised that we speak English back." They all laughed again, but Dody did not see the joke.

"You didn't answer my question," the boy said. "Aren't you afraid of us?"

Dody carefully weighed what his response ought to be. If he denied that he was afraid, the army of children might decide to do something to show how fearsome they could be. But if he admitted to his fear there was no telling what they might do to prove that he was right. He opened his mouth, ready to say that he was afraid, only to change his mind, shake his head and begin to declare that he wasn't frightened at all.

It was not just fear that paralyzed him, although

it was safe to say that Dody was frightened. But in all the time he had lived alone on the *Wanderer*, he never had to settle an argument, never quarreled with anyone and never had to fight for his beliefs. He had grown old without anyone to clash with. Now he wanted only to live peacefully within his own family, and to please everyone and anger no one. So he stood there like a doddering old hermit, unable to speak.

But Elaine didn't share his indecision. "Why should we be afraid of a bunch of little pipsqueaks like you?" she said.

"Then you aren't even a little afraid?" the boy asked. He was disappointed.

"That first one was afraid," said the girl with the golden hair. "It was funny the way he ran away so fast — wasn't it, Jonathan?"

"We scared him good," said the tall boy proudly. "But we wanted to catch him and take him to the budding grove."

"What's the budding grove?" Elaine asked.

"You'll see," said Jonathan. "We're going to take you there."

"Not unless we want to go," Elaine said.

"I guess you're from Earth," said the boy.

"Sure," said Elaine. "Aren't you?"

"No, but I think I'd like it there. Isn't it warm there?"

"In California it's warm most of the time," Elaine said.

"And it's wet, too — isn't it?"

"Parts are very wet," said Elaine.

"It's warm then *and* wet," Jonathan said. "I could tell by the look of you that it was warm and wet. Now I know I'd really like it there."

"Were you born here?" Dody asked.

All the children laughed.

"None of us were *born* here," Jonathan said. "We weren't *born* anywhere."

"They must've hatched," Elaine said to Dody.

"Not *hatched*, either," said Jonathan. "We're from the budding grove. You'll see when we take you."

Dody didn't like the sound of that. He didn't want to be taken anywhere by these children — if they *were* children.

There was something very different and very wrong about Jonathan and the others. They were just too perfect. For all their running about in the sun, they showed no signs of dirt or grime; no droplets of sweat ran down their foreheads or dampened their hair; no mud or dust soiled their coveralls. They were clean as newly washed white china. They were teacup clean, like no children Dody could remember from his own distant days back home.

They weren't people, Dody suddenly realized. They weren't *born* because they weren't people, but something else, even though they looked like people.

"Which way did Bobby go?" Elaine now asked, her anger rising. "Where did you chase our brother?"

"That other one, you mean?" Jonathan said. "By

now, he's probably been caught and taken to the budding grove." The boy stepped toward Elaine, playfully pointing his sword at her. "We're going to take you there, too."

"No way," said Elaine as she rushed up to Jonathan and easily knocked him down. His sword fell to the ground noiselessly, without even a clatter. She sat on the boy's heaving chest and pinned his arms to the ground with her knees. Totally at her mercy, he could only squirm in discomfort.

She had taken him by surprise but the advantage lasted only a minute or so. The rest of the crew soon rushed to the aid of their fallen comrade.

Dody stood frozen, arguing with himself again. He could not decide whether it was better to join Elaine in a hopeless fight or run for the lander while she served as a distraction. I'm just a little kid, he thought. Elaine won't expect me to help her. But then he reminded himself that he wasn't a kid anymore and that he ought to try to rescue his sister.

At first, Elaine seemed to have no difficulty taking very good care of herself. Still sitting on Jonathan, she was able to knock down one child after another, with ease, as they charged up to her. But they wouldn't stay down. And soon they surrounded her and began wrapping her in lengths of string that all of them carried looped over their shoulders. One length of string would not have held her, but twenty such loops all at once had her tied up in a tangle. She twisted and turned to pull herself free, but she could not hold them off for long by herself.

"Dody! Help me!"

Dody could stand still no longer. Without thinking, he rushed into the tornado of little people who were racing around his sister and began to knock them away. How light they seemed, as if they were made of bamboo or balsa wood, stuff far less substantial than muscle and bone. They began tossing lariats of string at him. The strands were made of a substance as sticky as a spider's thread but much thicker and very difficult to break. The string clung to him like chewing gum. His every movement was slowed by its grip.

Out of anger, he picked up Jonathan's fallen sword and soon he was batting children away with the toy weapon. Sword struck sword in a satisfying *th-wack*.

Oh, but he was happy for a minute or two. He felt as if he were young again. He had become Robin Hood, a knight of the Round Table, and a Musketeer, all in one, fighting against impossible odds. "Take that," he said aloud as his sword slapped against one of the children.

"Take that, and that," he said, just like a character in a movie or a book. But the army of children seemed to be enjoying the battle, too, and they did not give up. They soon surrounded him and struck at him from all sides. He swung his sword until his arms ached. Still, he might have won the battle single-handedly except for one rather disturbing accident.

Jonathan had snuck up on him from behind and kept poking him with the tip of a sword he'd taken from another boy.

It was not painful, but very bothersome to Dody, who turned around to fight off Jonathan face-to-face. He swung wildly, hitting the boy in the arm with all his strength. Dody's weapon was a mere toy, a piece of blunt wood, not a sharpened edge of metal. But the sword sliced through Jonathan's arm, like a knife carving through a joint of turkey. The blow sent half the boy's arm flying across the field of battle.

Dody was stunned at the sight of the severed limb. It lay on the ground, writhing, the hand clutching at the air as if trying to recover its sword.

Elaine continued to fight on, but Dody dropped his own toy weapon and stood in shock as the boys and girls of the child's army tied him up snugly with their string lariats, loop after loop, so that Dody was wound up in the sticky stuff. He couldn't move now if he'd wanted to. He stared at the severed arm, which continued to twitch with life. The children were free to gang up on Elaine, and they soon had her wrapped up in her own cocoon of string.

"I'm so sorry," Dody bleated as forty-eight or so hands, more or less, lifted them into the air. The army was going to carry the two of them away.

"So very, very sorry," Dody muttered as he managed to catch a look at Jonathan.

To Dody's surprise, the boy appeared to be in no

agony at all. In fact, he was smiling. No blood spurted from the stump of arm that the swipe of the wooden blade had left behind.

"He deserved it," Elaine said, trying to console her brother. "You gave the creep just what he was asking for."

"But I didn't mean to hurt him," Dody said. As if in response, the army of children stopped and placed Dody and Elaine on their feet on the ground. They stood side by side, unable to move arms or legs, like a pair of statues in a sculpture garden. "I didn't mean to hurt anybody."

"Of course you meant to or you wouldn't have been fighting," said one of the girls. "That's the fun of playing army. Once I whacked Roger's head off, and another time I lost three whole fingers from my left hand." Dody knew she was lying, because he could see that both her hands had all their fingers.

"Why be sorry?" Jonathan said. "I'd have done the same to you if you gave me the chance. It's just an arm."

"Aren't you in pain?" Elaine asked.

"I know the word, but I'm not sure I know what it means," Jonathan said. "Besides, there's no real harm."

He reached down to pick up the arm. He turned around, holding the arm up like a trophy for everyone to see. Dody was so horrified that he wanted to close his eyes, but the children applauded. Then Jonathan pushed the two cut ends of his severed arm together and held them there for a few seconds before he let go.

"As good as new," Jonathan said, snapping the fingers at the end of the restored arm to make the point. Dody was relieved. He began to see Jonathan in a new light. The boy was forgiving, almost kindly — as pleasant and agreeable as he was peculiar.

The other children laughed and shouted.

"They *are* munchkins," Elaine whispered to Dody.

"How did he do that?" asked Dody.

"You're very strange," Jonathan said.

"Not strange," said the girl with golden hair. "Stupid!"

"Not stupid," said Jonathan. "Ignorant!"

"Ignorant?" objected Elaine. "If I could move my hands, I'd give you a beating you wouldn't forget."

"And definitely ill-tempered," said the boy.

"I'm *not* ill-tempered!" Elaine insisted.

Dody knew he was right. Ignorant he certainly was and ill-tempered as well. The same could be said of his sister. After all, she was the one who struck the first blow. And what had the children done in response except defend themselves? Dody felt shame at his own actions.

And he might have said so in an attempt to make peace between the visitors from the planet Earth and these residents of planet 5, but then the ground on which they stood began quaking violently. Bound in a mass of sticky string, Dody could not keep his balance and fell to the ground. He landed so hard on his stomach that the breath was knocked out of him for a minute. He looked up as the ground continued to shake and buck beneath him. Elaine was also flat on the ground. They were both bobbing up and down as the ground rolled and swelled.

Dody knew a lot about earthquakes and had lived through many of them in California, including one that knocked jars and plates and books from their shelves and made long cracks in the plaster. But this was stronger than any earthquake he'd experienced. The children's army managed to stay on its feet, which was about as difficult as it would be to stay standing on the back of a running horse.

Then Dody noticed what was happening to the landing craft.

"Elaine!" he shouted. But there was no need to get her attention. She could see what was happening.

The edges of the cup of ground that had held the landing craft rose up around it. The tilted craft tumbled down the rising surface of planet 5 into what seemed like smacking lips. The crater had become a gigantic, yawning mouth, which engulfed and finally swallowed the lander entirely.

As suddenly as the quaking had begun, the ground stilled. For several seconds there was silence, which was broken by the sound of Elaine, not just sniffling or sobbing, but bawling.

"We'll never get home again! Never, ever!"

Dody wanted to comfort her, to assure her that

they would be rescued, returned to the spaceship *Wanderer* and their parents' keep. But he could not bring himself to say so. He was too forlorn himself to believe it. Well, at least he'd had a long life and had lived to see the sun again, even if it was not the same sun of his memories. But Elaine deserved more than this. He tried to turn his head to look at her, but the children were in the way now.

In a respectful silence, the army of children again lifted Dody and Elaine above their heads and began running so swiftly that Dody could feel a rush of wind through his hair.

"Where are we going?" Elaine shouted.

"To the budding grove," Jonathan yelled back at her.

"To the budding grove," called out the army of children.

SIX
THE BUDDING GROVE

"LOWER THEM EASY," Jonathan ordered the others. "Easy does it. The girl first. Then the old guy."

The others obeyed Jonathan's every order. He was taller than the rest and handsome. The other children seemed eager to do whatever pleased him. Bobby was that way, too, Dody thought — the sort of kid that thought of games for other kids to play, that other kids would want to follow.

Still bound up, Dody was handed from child to child, like baggage on a conveyor belt, down an oversized hole that pierced the drab surface of the planet. Jonathan made sure that they were not dropped or jostled as they descended into the shadowy tunnel. At first, Dody welcomed the cool moistness underground. It was a relief after the ride in the hot sun. He and Elaine were carried along a path that twisted and turned, rose and fell, dividing again

88

and again as Dody and Elaine rode deeper and deeper into the interior of the planet. The corridor was dimly lit so that at first they could hardly see, and as the tunnel narrowed the air became putrid and suffocatingly close.

"We'll have to stop and unbind them now," Jonathan said. "They're too big a load for the deeper passageways."

"Won't they run away?" asked the girl with the golden hair.

"Not if they want to get out ever again." Jonathan saw to it that they were lowered gently to the ground and not tossed or dropped.

It took a minute or so for Dody's eyes to adjust to the faint light that shone from the walls of the tunnel. He saw Jonathan pull a pair of scissors from a sheath sewn into his coveralls. With the hand that had been so recently rejoined to his body, the boy began cutting deftly through the sticky strings that covered Dody.

"I don't think you'll try to escape," he said to Dody as he worked to cut him free. "I'll make sure that nothing happens to harm you."

"I don't believe this," Elaine said. "They kidnap us and now they want us to think that they won't hurt us."

"Just get us out of this stuff," Dody said. "Please."

"*You* can beg all you want, Dody," Elaine said. "But *I* won't."

"You'd never find your way out by yourself,

Elaine," Dody said, alarmed that they might be separated. "We need to stick together."

"We could make sure that you stick together," said a little red-haired girl, twirling her lariat of gummy string. The others laughed at the joke.

Elaine tried to ignore them.

"I suppose you're right," she said quietly. "He can untie me, too," she said.

"Terrific!" Dody said.

The army of children giggled, repeating again and again, "Terrific. Terrific. Terrific."

"It means 'frightening,' doesn't it?" Jonathan asked.

"Only some of the time," Dody said. "What I meant was 'great,' 'fine' or 'splendid.' "

"So many opposite meanings," Jonathan said. "I wonder if I'll ever learn to understand you."

Jonathan finished snipping Dody free. Dody rose stiffly to his feet, his joints popping as he moved, his limbs tingling.

In the moonglow dimness of light, he watched Jonathan work the scissors, snip by snip, until Elaine was free, too. Even in the faint glimmer, Dody could see the boy's full smile splitting the pale roundness of his face. He was enjoying the game he was playing.

But Dody was still frightened. He wondered what the children had in mind for them next. Where was the "budding grove" and what was in store for them once they got there? He didn't like the sound of it. But if he and Elaine ran away there was nowhere they could go without risking being lost in the tunnels forever. Jonathan was right about that. Dody and Elaine were untied, but they weren't free.

One by one, most of the children's army had disappeared down the tunnel, leaving Elaine and Dody alone with Jonathan.

"Where are they going?" Elaine asked.

"You'll see," Jonathan said. "Just follow me."

He began walking, and they had no choice but to follow. He took them through passages that turned and twisted and branched repeatedly. The ground was moist and even a little slippery. They were so deep underground that the pale, greenish light could not have come from the alien sun that baked the surface of the planet. The walls glowed with a radiance of their own, like lightning bugs, with a pale phosphorescence.

They continued downward for a little way before coming to a wall that appeared to block them from going any further. But Jonathan simply pushed against it, opening the way. After they had all passed through, Jonathan released the barrier and it sprang back into place. They passed through many such doorways as they walked for hours in a grim silence. Dody soon realized just how difficult it would be to find their way out of the maze of tunnels. He had long ago lost track of the branches they had taken.

The passages reminded him of blood vessels, twisting and dividing; the fleshy barriers were like valves. He shuddered at the comparison.

Jonathan moved ahead steadily, confident of his

direction, leaving Dody and Elaine to scamper to keep up. They were getting tired.

"Where are you taking us?" Elaine said sharply, when she felt too tired to go any further.

"I'm taking you to our leader, naturally," said Jonathan, who stopped for the first time since the three of them had begun walking. "And then I'll show you the budding grove just like I promised."

"How much further?"

"Just a little way."

"When will we get there?"

"We'll be there pretty soon," Jonathan said. His voice, Dody realized, was as odd as the rest of him. It was a younger kid's voice, not like Bobby's, which cracked and squeaked sometimes. Its tone was as clear and true as a note on an organ pipe, a perfect voice. Like everything else about Jonathan, it was too perfect to be real. "Pretty soon," he had said, just the way any kid would have said it. Not "very soon" or "presently" or "shortly," the way a parent might have, but "pretty soon." Like a regular boy, but somehow not quite.

Jonathan began walking again with long, quick strides that would have soon left his companions behind.

"Can't we rest just for a minute?" Elaine said. "I'm tired."

"I'm *never* tired," Jonathan said. "But I should've let you rest. We can sit here a few minutes, if you want to." Elaine and Dody hunkered down but did not actually sit on the wet, slimy floor of the tunnel. Jonathan followed their example.

"You aren't human, are you?" Elaine asked.

"We are Errat," said Jonathan.

"A rat?" she asked.

"Errat," Jonathan repeated, patiently. "It's the name we use for this place and those of us who live in it."

"How did your family get here?" Dody asked. "Did they come in a spaceship like ours?"

"We're travelers like you, but we didn't have a spaceship," Jonathan said. "Errat didn't need a spaceship, not then. We sailed across space on a wind of light, looking for a place that was warm and wet. It was warm and wet here then. You can see how it's changed. Down here it's warm and wet all the time, but everywhere else, up on top, it's hot and dry."

"Were you here when the first spaceship came?" Dody asked.

"Errat was here then," Jonathan said. "But not me. Not yet."

"So you *were* born here," Elaine said.

"I was *made* here, not born. In the budding grove, where all the rest of us were made. You'll see."

"I'm not sure I want to," Elaine said.

"What happened to the ship?" Dody asked. "What happened to the people from Earth?" Like the *Wanderer*, the first ships of the migration were full of adults and children. The scientist Hoffman should

93

have been among them. It had been his beacon they were following. "What happened to them all?" Dody asked.

Without answering, Jonathan rose to his feet and began walking quickly down the tunnel again. "I'll show you," he said as the others scrambled to keep up with him.

After a few turns and branches, they turned into a larger passage that opened up into a rounded chamber the size of a school gymnasium. Glistening struts crisscrossed the space, giving it support. Even here in the great hollow cavern of a room, the walls glowed with light. Moisture dripped from every surface. A nasty drop hit Dody's forehead. It was a thick, almost gooey substance, more like spit than water, and he wished that he could wash it away.

The room was like the chamber of a heart. His fourth-grade teacher had shown the class a cow's heart, sliced open just like any piece of meat. But inside a wall of thick muscles were flappy pockets and surprising hollows, the larger ones full of struts and columns. This central chamber was like that, like an empty heart that had been drained of all blood, its movement stilled. But it was warm and wet. And it still seemed very much alive.

There were hundreds of children bustling in and out of the chamber. The place was teeming with them. They were all too busy to pay any attention to Dody and Elaine.

"Is this the budding grove?" Elaine asked.

"No, you'll see that later," Jonathan said. "Now I want you to meet Walter."

From the middle of a cluster of children, a small, hunched figure of a man moved toward them. He wore a hooded cape that was covered in brown fibers like a coconut shell. The hump on his back was almost as large as he was. He glided toward them, as if he were skating across the floor.

Jonathan immediately threw himself to his knees, placing his head on the ground while thrusting his arms up toward Walter. "May Errat live forever," he said.

"Forever," Walter said in a gasping whisper of a voice.

"I've brought you visitors," Jonathan said as he rose to a kneeling position.

"I can see." The creature pulled the hood back from his head. Dody saw a withered little face. It was dark and shriveled as if it had been left in the sun to dry like an apricot.

His mouth was puckered, and he seemed to have difficulty stretching it into a smile. His face was twisted to one side, all wrinkles and bulges on one half, taut and smooth on the other. Even his pointed, yellow teeth seemed small and shrunken.

"Pleased to meet you," Walter said. He spoke as if he were in the middle of an asthma attack and needed to take a breath after every word or two.

"Pleased to meet you, too, Walter," Elaine said, walking toward him and extending her hand. Before

95

she could reach him, the tiny man scuddered away like a cockroach.

"No touching!" he screamed. "Absolutely no touching!" Jonathan by this time was on his feet, standing protectively between Elaine and the little personage.

"He's very, very fragile," Jonathan explained. "It would be too dangerous to touch him. He's not ready."

"I didn't mean to hurt him," Elaine said. "Is he your leader?"

"He's 'the one among many,'" Jonathan said. "He was like the rest of us and then he changed."

The little man opened his mouth as if to speak, but coughed instead. A dry puff of dust exploded from his mouth.

"You must help us," Walter said at last.

Dody realized he was beginning to like Jonathan, but Walter made him feel on edge again, as if he were in the presence of a mortal enemy.

"The others before you," Walter said, "they couldn't help us. We must leave this place. Before the wetness is gone. Before heat overtakes us. But their ship was crippled. We've been waiting for you. Now you can help us."

"We're stranded ourselves," Dody said.

The little man coughed again, filling the air with dust as fine as talcum powder. The smell of it was foul, like a mold on cottage cheese left in the re-frigerator too long. Elaine began madly waving the air to keep from breathing it. Alarmed at the sudden movement, Walter backed away.

A swarm of children surrounded him, as if to protect him from her.

"The others will come for you," Walter said, once he was safe from Elaine's reach. "The beacon will bring them, and they will take us with them."

"Where do you want to go?" Dody asked.

"Wherever you live, there can we flourish," Walter said. "Wherever it's warm and wet."

"We won't take you with us!" Elaine blurted out. "Not on your life!"

"Then," Walter said, his mouth too shriveled and puckered to show any feeling, "you can't go, either."

"We're prisoners, Dody," said Elaine. "They're holding us hostage."

She began moving toward Walter, and the crowd of children closed in even more tightly around him.

"I am weary," Walter said. He began backing away. His dark, sunken eyes watched Elaine as he moved toward a wall. "So very weary," he said as a giant flap of wall opened up behind him. It closed again with a sudden, fleshy snap, and Walter had vanished.

Within seconds, all the children except Jonathan had disappeared from the chamber. Dody was relieved that Walter was gone.

"Is Bobby a prisoner, too?" Elaine asked. Alone with just Jonathan and Dody, she seemed small and frightened.

"I don't know where Bobby is," Jonathan said. "He might be in the budding grove."

"Then take us there," she said. "Right away."

"Follow me," Jonathan said.

As they walked along hurriedly behind the tall boy, Dody could hear Elaine crying. She could be far braver than he could, but she was still a young girl.

"I'm sorry that I got us into this mess," Dody said.

"You couldn't know what would happen," she said.

"I'm a big disappointment to you," he said glumly. "You wanted me to be the way I was, and now you're disappointed."

"I miss the way you were," Elaine confessed. She began crying even more loudly.

"You can't turn the clock back, you know," Dody said, pulling his crumpled bandana from a pocket and offering it to her. She refused to take it from him.

Elaine took Dody's hand and for a second the pair slowed, not trying to keep up with Jonathan, who was striding way ahead.

"I know we can't change things," she said. "But wouldn't it be nice if we could? I wish we'd never left the earth and things were the way they always were."

Dody didn't answer. A part of him wished that they'd never rocketed off into space, but another part was glad they had, even if it had not turned out the way it was supposed to. Even if he'd known what would happen, would he have changed things? He didn't think so.

They raced to catch up with Jonathan, slipping in their haste on the slick ground. By the time they caught up with him, they were breathless, but they did not want to be left behind underground in the fetid damp of a labyrinth.

They would have to trust Jonathan to keep his promise to protect them from harm.

After they'd walked for what seemed like an hour, Jonathan began racing far ahead of them, disappearing down a long corridor, nowhere to be seen.

Dody and Elaine began running until they came to a dead end in the passageway. They could hear a muted shout from the other side of a great fleshy wall. "In here," the voice said. They pressed against the wall.

It opened like a giant mouth and devoured them whole.

They were deposited, unharmed, into a sizable room. Side by side were dozens of slabs, arranged like beds in a dormitory.

Jonathan's excited, high-pitched voice startled them. "I promised you I'd show you the budding grove."

"So?" said Elaine. "Looks like summer camp to me."

"This is where I came from," Jonathan explained. "I was copied here."

"Copied from what?" Elaine wanted to know.

"From a boy who came on the first ship," he said. "You could be copied, too. Then you'd be part of Errat, like me."

"No way," Elaine said.

Dody was so exhausted that he sat on one of the slabs. But he looked at Jonathan with a new appreciation. Just as Dody had thought, the boy was not a real person, but a copy, an ersatz child. And yet he looked and behaved, not like a mannikin or robot, but like a genuine human being.

Dody was so sleepy that he stretched out on the slab bed. He felt relaxed now in the budding grove, as if every worry had been taken from him. Dozing, he thought for a moment he was riding the waves at his favorite beach in California, bobbing up and down under a hot sun in the cool water. It was warm and wet there. The surf was gentle, pushing him toward land and then tugging him out to sea again. He wished his dream could go on forever and ever.

Elaine screamed. "Dody, get up!"

She reached out a hand to him and pulled him roughly from the slab. "Look," she said. "You were sinking down."

He could see the impression his body left behind in the bed of clay that had grown soft as mud. It was a mold ready to be filled. Dody wasn't sure how.

"You could be like me," Jonathan said. "We'd have fun together, the three of us."

"What happened to the boy?" Dody demanded. "The one you were copied from?"

"The same as happened to all the others," he said. "He's mostly gone."

"Mostly?" asked Elaine.

Jonathan reached into a pocket of his coveralls. "Except for these," he said. "Errat always leaves these." Dody reached out to take the small white objects from Jonathan's outstretched hand.

"What are they?" Elaine asked.

Dody rattled them together like dice in his hand. "They're teeth," he said. "Human teeth."

SEVEN
SEARCHING FOR HOFFMAN

THE TEETH WERE SMOOTH and white, without a cavity.

"They could be Bobby's teeth," Elaine said.

"They're not." Jonathan tried to calm her.

"I'm scared of this place," Elaine said.

"There's nothing to be *scared* of," Jonathan said. "You tell her, Dody. Were *you* scared just now?"

Dody shook his head. He hadn't been frightened at all. "I was having a wonderful dream," he said.

"You should've been scared," Elaine said. "If I didn't save you, you would have been dead like everyone on the first spaceship." Dody knew that she was right. If she hadn't reached for him he would have sunk into the mud and been replaced by something else. A copy. Only his teeth would have been left, like so many stones. He shuddered to think what might have happened.

Elaine turned to Jonathan in a fury. "*You* would have been afraid if someone had tried to do that to you."

"I'm not like you," Jonathan said. For the first time, he looked unhappy. "I've never been afraid. It makes me very sad that I upset you. But it's great to be a copy. We don't get old, you know. We play all the time and never get tired. There are no grown-ups around to tell us what to do."

"Then none of the grown-ups were copied," Dody said.

"Only the children were," said the boy. "The grown-ups never came here. They looked, but they never found the budding grove. And we didn't want them here."

"Then Hoffman could still be alive," Dody said.

"He'd know how to find Bobby," Elaine said.

"And help us get back to the *Wanderer*," said Dody. "He might even have a landing craft or rocket."

"I've never heard of Hoffman," Jonathan said. "But if he's alive, I know where to find him. All of the old ones live together in a place far from here."

"Can you show us how to get there?" Dody asked.

The smile returned to Jonathan's face. "Sure I can show you," he said. "Better than that, I can take you there myself. Getting there is dangerous, and you'd probably get lost. Let me take you."

"I don't trust him," said Elaine.

"Would you rather stay here and wait for the

other children to catch us?" Dody asked her.

She looked around at the damp, dimly lit room with its slab beds laid out in a row, one after another, like tombs.

"Take us to Hoffman," she ordered Jonathan, and the boy went racing from the budding grove so fast that the other two had trouble keeping up with him.

After the three of them had been clambering steadily up steep passageways for more than an hour, Dody had begun to doubt that they would ever see sunlight again. As they walked in the foul, humid air of the tunnels, he found his thoughts wandering to other places and other times. In his mind he began writing a letter to Tony and Alan.

I keep wishing I could go to the beach again. I'd swim until I was so cold that my lips would turn purple. Then I'd come out and lie on the warm sand and let my bones bake in the sun. And when I was warm enough, I'd go back in the waves again.

It feels like we've been walking forever. Sometimes I feel like I can't get enough air or that I won't ever see the sunshine again. So I think about beaches. I'm sure there are beaches here on this planet. From the lander we could see deserts running down to the sea. There are moons to pull the tide and winds to pile up waves on the water. There have to be beaches.

He jogged ahead to catch up with Jonathan. He grabbed him by the arm. "Are there beaches here?"

"I don't know the word *beaches*," the boy said.

"You don't know much," Elaine said as she

caught up with the other two. "I wonder if you know your way out of this anthill."

"A *beach* is a place where ocean water washes over sand," Dody explained more patiently.

"Of course, we have beaches, then," Jonathan said. "But I'd never go there."

"Why not? Water too cold?" Elaine asked.

"Yes, it's cold, but that's not why. The ocean is too salty. If I went in the water, I'd shrivel up like a raisin."

"Is that what made old Walter all shrunken and wrinkled?" Elaine asked.

"No, that's not it." Jonathan laughed. "He's about to spore."

"Spore?" Elaine asked. "It sounds disgusting."

"Spores are like seeds," Dody said. "Like the under side of a mushroom. But people don't spore."

"You saw that hump on Walter's back, didn't you?" said the boy. "That was his spore pod. After a while it'll break open and the spores will scatter everywhere."

"And what will happen to Walter?" Elaine asked.

"There'll be nothing left," Jonathan said.

"Poor guy," Elaine said. "He was cute in his way. He looked like one of those dried-up apple-head dolls."

"He's 'the one among many.' One of us is always getting ready to spore. It's supposed to be an honor to be the one who's sporing."

"Some honor," she said. "To pop open like a

105

puffball." Back home in the woods, she and Dody liked to find the ball-shaped funguses and squeeze them until they burst in a puff of dust.

"What happens to the spores?" Dody asked.

"They'll grow," the boy said. "They'll keep Errat alive forever."

Dody wanted to know more, but before he could ask another question, he felt a warm, dry breeze whisk down upon them, bringing with it a wonderful, flowered fragrance. He charged ahead of the other two, until he finally broke into the blinding sunshine. Puffing and gasping, he stopped to catch his breath, but it stayed just out of grasp. His lungs, his chest, his belly, his whole torso worked furiously to get enough air. When he was a boy that little run would have been nothing; now it left him wheezing and clutching at his throat with every breath.

His eyes had adjusted enough to begin surveying the landscape when Elaine and Jonathan finally caught up with him. He hoped to spot another of the ship's landing craft or some other sign of his parents. But all around him was nothing but the faintly green landscape of the featureless plain.

His parents should have been there by now, Dody thought. *They* should have found a way to rescue their children by now. His parents had failed him. Now he would have to turn to someone else.

"How do we get to Hoffman?" he asked.

"He's out there," said Jonathan, pointing across the plain. "It will be a long way, over the sands."

"What are we waiting for?" said Dody.

"I'm not going anywhere until I get something to eat and something to drink," Elaine stated emphatically.

Dody realized that he was hungry, too. He searched the pockets of his coveralls, but there was no tube of food, no bottle of juice to be found.

"Oh, I can take care of that," Jonathan said. He pulled out his scissors, plucked up the skin of the planet and made an incision. He reached into the cut he had made and pulled out a handful of greenish pulp. "Thanks to Errat, giver of life," he said and then began to eat the jellylike stuff. "Try some."

"Ugh!" said Elaine, as if he had offered her liver and onions. "I'm not *that* hungry or thirsty!"

But Dody was that hungry and thirsty. He reached into the cut with a large hand and brought out a pawful. "It's really very good," he said after a few nibbles. "Like a peach."

The wound Jonathan had made now began filling with a greenish fluid. "It's the nectar," Jonathan said, using his hand like a cup to bring some of the liquid to his mouth. "It's the best part."

"Oh, gore!" Elaine said. "It's gross. Like drinking green blood."

Again, Dody was willing to try it. "It's minty," he said. "And carbonated." He tried some more.

Elaine, too, was finally thirsty enough to give the drink a try. "It's like soda pop," she said, and took handful after handful to her mouth.

The liquid continued to spill from the cut in the planet surface, much faster then they could drink it, so that it formed a rounded pool. Soon the edges of the spring were covered with a crust of a darker green that grew toward the center of the pool.

"Yuck!" said Elaine, now that she had satisfied her thirst. "It's clotting."

"Of course," said Jonathan. "If the nectar kept running forever, Errat would wither and die. First, she satisfies our thirst and our hunger, then she heals up the wound we made."

"Miraculous," Dody said. He marveled that to Jonathan the planet itself was a being, a giant goddess that nourished the lesser creatures that walked upon her.

"Gory!" Elaine persisted. "Now, can we get going? I want to find Bobby. Take us to Hoffman."

"To Hoffman," said Dody.

"To Hoffman," said Jonathan, who led them over the spongy ground. "We need to walk toward where the sun sets."

"Westward, ho!" Dody said. He walked with a bounce to his step only partly explained by the springiness of the earth. The heat did not bother him, nor did the monotony of the view, broken here and there by a dark green scar where he assumed that other travelers had partaken of Errat's nectar and flesh.

The three travelers moved on steadily for hours until the ground, which had been so flat, began to fall away sharply, down to a land of red dunes and dusty swirls, the vast desert of planet 5.

"Ur-Errat," said Jonathan. "That's what we call it, the 'land that was, before Errat.' It was a beautiful place once. Now it's dangerous. There's no food to eat and nothing to drink. It's dry and hot."

"A red desert," Dody proclaimed. "We saw it from the landing craft. But it seems so much larger here."

"I hope we don't have to cross over it," said Elaine. "My feet are sore already. I must have a blister on every toe."

"We don't have to cross it, not all of it," Jonathan assured her. "But we do have to walk out on it. But not right away. We need to wait until night, when the air's cooler. And then we'll have to watch out for the Winnems."

"What are Winnems?" Elaine asked.

"They're fearsome creatures that live out on the desert. They were here even before Errat ever came. They don't like strangers at all. They're our enemies."

"They sound like the Indians," Elaine said.

"Indians?" Jonathan was puzzled again.

"The native people back on Earth, in America," Dody said. "I'll bet the Winnems didn't like having their lands taken from them anymore than the Indians liked losing theirs back at home."

"We couldn't help that," Jonathan said. "Errat needed room to grow. And anyway, they're nasty people. They can make the most terrifying sounds."

"Maybe we're better off waiting for Bobby underground," Elaine said.

"I'd rather take a chance on being eaten up on the desert than to go back in those tunnels again," said Dody. "And we have to find Hoffman. Even if he doesn't know where Bobby is, he's a genius. He'll know how to get us back to the *Wanderer*."

Jonathan made another incision in the planet skin and drew out more food and nectar. Elaine and Dody were so hungry and dry that they filled themselves to bursting. Then they napped until almost sunset, getting up in time to watch the purple rays of an alien sun. From the slopes of Errat, they could see the swirling whirlwinds of desert dust rising in the distance.

Jonathan did not seem to need sleep. He stood the whole time, as night fell and the first stars began to appear.

At last a pair of half-moons, small and silver, rose up in the sky, touching the desert with their pallid light. "We have five moons," Jonathan explained. "These two we call the doublet. The other bigger ones follow later on. It's a good idea to begin now, when there's light enough for us to travel but not enough for our enemies to see us."

It was surprisingly difficult to walk down the steep slope without falling, so they slid down on the seats of their coveralls until they reached the desert dunes. Although the air was cool now, almost chilly, the sand still radiated the heat of the day. The going was slower, as their feet sunk into the sand and their path took them up dunes several stories high and then down again into sandy valleys.

"I'm thirsty," Elaine said. Dody's mouth was thick with dust and sand, but there was nothing to drink on the desert, away from the living surface of Errat. Here the land was dry and dead. They walked along ever more slowly, the twin moons casting faint, double shadows across the sands.

"I'm very thirsty," Elaine said again after they had walked over another dune. "Aren't we ever going to stop?"

Dody was surprised that his sister would behave like such a little kid, but he did not have the energy to quarrel with her.

"We have a long way to go," Jonathan said, giving Elaine no comfort at all. "We can't stop now, while we still have the doublet moons to travel by."

Dody had seen Jonathan look up from time to time, using the stars to guide them across the strange, forbidding landscape of Ur-Errat. It was an alien sky above them, of glowing planets and twinkling stars in unfamiliar combinations. On Earth, Dody could pick out Polaris, the North Star, from all the others. And he supposed that here, too, there were guide-stars that allowed Jonathan to keep them on their course as they crossed the rolling desert.

The first of the double moons fell below the horizon quickly followed by the second. When they dropped, it was as if someone turned up the power of the stars, so bright did they shine against the pure blackness of the universe behind them. A wide smudge of light across the sky was surely the same Milky Way that Dody had known as a boy on Earth.

Jonathan hunched down as they neared the top of a dune. "We have to stop now and wait for the Mother Moon," he said. "It won't be long." The air was cooler now and a faint breeze rose from the direction of their travel. Dody lay back in the warm sand. He could hear Elaine's deep breathing as she settled into sleep, but Jonathan sat rigidly near the crest of the dune, vigilant and waiting.

"You seem worried," Dody said.

"I know there are dangers here, but I don't know where they'll come from," Jonathan said. "It's a good idea to lie low and be quiet."

Dody could not sleep. He found himself shaking. His life had been lonely, but in its monotony it had been totally predictable. Now he could not be sure what might happen. He lifted up onto his elbows and listened for danger. And when he finally heard a noise, it was unexpected and earthly, like the hum of a high voltage line across the desert. What followed was unmistakable: the sound of Elaine, not screaming but terribly frightened.

"Oh. Oh. Oh," she said. "What is it? What's on me?"

She was on her feet, jumping and shaking as if she were dancing to fast music. "Get them off," she pleaded. "Dody, help me get them off me."

He leaped up and scrambled down toward her. Every inch of Elaine was covered with a silvery, seething crust of tiny insects that shone in the soft glow of stars. Jonathan rushed to help. They brushed and swatted at a mass of swarming life that covered Elaine. Large pieces of the stuff dropped off, clots that fell and dissolved into the sand.

The earth hummed and sizzled beneath their feet as the shiny clumps scattered and disappeared into the dune.

And then there was an awful silence, complete and alarming, as if even their lungs and hearts had for the moment stopped to rest.

"I'm OK. I'm OK," Elaine said at last. "Ooo, that was awful. What could they be? They were like insects, but smaller than insects. And so many of them, billions of them, all over me."

Dody shuddered. "Did they hurt you?" he asked.

"That's what was so strange. It didn't hurt a bit. Maybe I was too scared to hurt. What were they, Jonathan?"

"They wouldn't hurt you, because you're still alive," the boy explained. "They're called scourers. They're everywhere, but you just don't see them. The smallest movement can frighten them away. They're not interested in anything alive. They're scavengers. They scour this planet for things that aren't alive. They eat the dead."

"What's that smell?" Elaine brought her hands to

her nose and sniffed them suspiciously. "Can you smell it, Dody?"

"It's strange," he said. "Like overripe fruit."

"It's from them," Elaine said. "From those little creepy things. I'm covered with their awful smell. I wish I could take a bath. How do I look? I must look terrible. I wish I was home. Let's get away from here, before they come back again."

Dody held Elaine close to him and stroked her hair. "Everything will be all right," he found himself saying, as if he were his own father. "You'll be fine, just fine."

Jonathan put a hand on each of their heads and stroked them. "Don't worry," he said. "I'll get you to Hoffman. I promise."

At last, a huge moon rose above a distant dune. Like the doublet, it was only half illuminated, a half-moon but so large that the desert became visible under its silver light.

"This way," Jonathan said. Instead of climbing to the top of each dune, he lead them instead through valleys and depressions. Although this winding course lengthened the distance they would have to travel, it kept them away from ridges. "I don't want us to be so visible," he said.

Dody was feeling his sixty years. His legs were leaden, almost as hard to move as the limbs of the toy knights he had left behind on Earth.

"Couldn't we stop for a minute?" he asked.

"I'm tired, too," Elaine asserted.

"I forgot that you get tired so easily," Jonathan said. "We can rest for a while."

In the quiet of a valley between two dunes, with the half-moon directly over their heads, they stopped. They were too fearful now to lie down in the sand and sleep, but crouched down and cramped, they got what rest they could.

Again an unexpected noise broke the stillness. It was muted at first but quickly grew louder and louder. It was unmistakably the sound of hooves in the sand, hundreds of them.

"The Winnems," Jonathan said. "Don't say a word."

Closer and closer came the hoofbeats. "Oh, I hope they don't find us," Elaine said.

She'd spoken too loudly. The pounding hooves stopped. Dody was the first to look up. At the top of both dunes stood hundreds of tall, sturdy figures. They looked like men, but they seemed larger than men. They were two-legged creatures covered with shaggy fur. As they ran down the dunes toward the valley where the three trespassers were crouched, their hooves pounded the desert ground and their long manes flew behind them. The ones in the lead whinnied to the rest, as if ordering them into formation. They swept down in two great Vs over the hills of sand. As they neared, Dody could see that their faces were bare, their mouths pulled back, their eyebrowless eyes wide open and wild. Perhaps by day they would have seemed less formidable, but in the moonlight and shadows of the desert valley, they were an invincible calvary, relentlessly stampeding upon a helpless enemy.

Dody fully expected to be trampled to death. "We're finished," he said. He felt as if he had risen above the scene and could view it at a calm distance. He wasn't frightened at all.

"Do something, Dody," Elaine said. "You're the grown-up. Do something!"

Dody wondered what his father would do with hundreds of Winnems racing toward them but could think of nothing.

Sand was everywhere. Waves of it washed over their legs and clouds of it filled the air with a choking dust. The sound of hooves and the whinnying and snorting of all those equine creatures made a terrific din. Dody could smell their pungent animal smell.

He did not see the one who knocked him to the ground, because he was watching another of the beasts pick up Elaine and throw her with ease over a shoulder. She wriggled and kicked to no avail. "Help me, Dody!" she shouted.

Dody wanted to curl up on the ground, to protect himself at all costs. But the cry of his sister in peril propelled him to his feet, and he charged at the Winnem who held her. The animal-man simply tossed Dody to one side, as easily as a stevedore might toss a sack of grain into a ship's hold. Jonathan threw himself into the fight, clinging to the Winnem with his arms and legs and teeth. The creature ignored him, galloping back up the dune at a furious pace with all the others following him. "Pick on someone your own size!" Elaine yelled. Near the crest, Jonathan lost his grip and fell to the sand.

As suddenly as they had appeared, the Winnems vanished, carrying Elaine with them. The sounds of hooves and whinnying quickly faded. Dody picked himself up very gingerly, testing one limb at a time for damage. His ribs ached from their collision with the earth. He might have broken one or two. But he limped up to the crest where Jonathan still lay. The boy's body was a heap in the sand, limp as a scarecrow pulled down from its stakes.

Dody felt he was about to cry.

"Jonathan, are you all right?"

One of the boy's arms stirred, then another. His body uncurled, his limbs stiffened, he sat up, he stood. "Are you hurt?" Dody asked.

"I think I'm fine," Jonathan said. "Didn't hurt a bit."

"You were amazing," Dody said. "I didn't know you had it in you."

"I surprised myself," the boy admitted. "I'm not sure what came over me."

"You were angry, Jonathan," Dody said.

"It's not a way I've ever felt before."

"Sometimes, it's fine to be angry," Dody said. He was angry himself, but also more frightened than ever.

From where they stood at the crest of the dune,

they could see the tracks made by the herd of Winnems, who were already far away and out of view. Their path veered slightly to the north.

"We need to follow them," Dody said.

"That would be stupid," Jonathan said. "What would we do if we caught them? They outnumber us. They're bigger and stronger. And cruel. We'd better find Hoffman. He'll be able to help us. He can't be very far away."

Dody felt a burden had been taken away from him. Of course, Hoffman would rescue them if anyone could. "Let's find Hoffman," Dody agreed. "Hoffman can take care of everything."

They walked around the base of a giant dune and saw a larger one looming above them, and another even larger one still beyond that.

They traveled until the half-moon dropped below the largest of the dunes. The valley was dark and cool, the heat of the day gone from the sand. Crouching down, the two travelers huddled together to warm one another.

"Do you think we'll ever get out of here?" Jonathan asked.

"Sure," Dody said, although he was not at all sure.

"Tell me about Earth," the boy said. "Are there sand dunes like this on Earth?"

"Lots of them," Dody said. "My family would go camping on the desert in the spring sometimes. We'd go for walks on the dunes. You couldn't see many animals, but you'd see snake and lizard tracks across the sand where they'd been crawling. At night it would be cold just like this and we'd stay up playing games and telling stories in our tent. No Winnems there to worry about. Nothing to worry about except a rattlesnake now and then. Nothing to worry about at all inside the tent."

"I wish I had a family," Jonathan said. "Not just other kids, but a mother and a father like you have."

"But you've got all those others," Dody said. "It must be like having hundreds of brothers and sisters. A mob of friends."

"It's not the same," the boy said. "Not at all."

Dody's teeth chattered in the cold. He felt anew the pain of waking up on the giant ship before all the others.

"I was alone for so very long," Dody said. "I waited so long for my family, and now I'm all alone again."

"You're not *all* alone," Jonathan said.

"No, you're right," Dody said, looking at the boy's eyes gleaming in the starlight. "I've got one friend with me at least."

All at once, the sand began hissing and crawling beneath them. They ran to escape being swept downward by a river of moving sand. It was as if they were charging up a down escalator. But the flow of sand soon overwhelmed them and carried them down so fast that they began tumbling and rolling.

When the falling ended, Dody was sitting upright

on a flat bed of sand in total darkness. To his surprise, his landing had been soft and he was uninjured. "Jonathan?" he called.

"Here," said the boy. When Dody reached out he found the boy's tousled hair. All but his head had been buried in sand. Bone-tired, Dody moved as quickly as he could to clear the sand away and then lay panting on the ground.

Then a voice beckoned them. "This way, this way." It was an old and tremulous voice, a grandfatherly voice that was friendly and reassuring.

EIGHT
In the Cave of
the Old Ones

Dody and Jonathan got to their feet and groped toward the speaker whom they couldn't see. They heard the sound of a key in a lock, of a bolt moving, metal against metal, and then they saw a shaft of light as a gargantuan door opened just a crack into a lighted room. The door was round, and the light took the shape of a crescent moon. "Give a hand please, give a hand," the voice now said. "I'm not as young as I used to be."

In the strong light and dark shadow, Dody could begin to make out the owner of the voice. He was an old man, dressed in a robe of coarse cloth, like a medieval monk might wear. His head was bare, and his hair stood up in tufts, grayer even than Dody's. Grabbing the metallic door with his gnarled hands, he gave his entire weight to opening it further. Dody and Jonathan joined him. "Not too much, not too much," the old man said. "We'll only have to shut it again. Just open it enough to let you squeeze through."

Once inside, they pushed the door shut behind them. They were in a small, well-lighted room with bowed metallic walls. At the far end was a doorway that opened into a long corridor.

"Very good, very good," the old man said, rubbing his hands together.

He stared at Dody and Jonathan and they stared back at him. He was a remarkable figure, almost as tall as Dody, but years older and bent with age. His eyes were more gray than blue, like a winter sky. His eyebrows were dark brown and bushy punctuation marks that gave his face a rather surprised expression.

"Dear, dear," the old man said. "You," he pointed in Jonathan's direction, "aren't allowed. I'll have to put you out again."

"If he goes, then I go," Dody said.

"But he's one of them, don't you see?" the old man said. "He's likely to cause problems for us all here. It won't do to let him in. You never know what one of *them* might be up to."

"He's my friend," Dody said.

"That may be, that may be," the old man said. "But still we haven't allowed it."

"Then we'll have to search for Bobby and Elaine by ourselves, without any help from Hoffman," Dody said, turning to the door.

"Oh, please," the old man said. "I suppose we might make an exception just this one time. But, you see, I've never heard of a friendship between one of us and one of them before."

"It's all right," Jonathan said sadly. "What he says is true. My other friends say it's a mistake to become friendly with one of you. We're supposed to keep our distance."

"We're different," Dody said. "But you're still my friend."

"Maybe you don't understand just how different they are, young man," the old man said. "Their form is all right, it's their substance that isn't. After a while you can pick it up at a glance. They're a little too clean, a little too tidy. They're greaseless. No oil glands. Gives them a different finish from ours. They're friendly enough, most of them, I grant you that. Yet they're not *us*. They're ersatz, and it won't do to forget that. For now, I suppose he can come along, if you insist. There's no harm as long as we keep a close eye on him. This way, this way."

Dody and Jonathan followed the old man, whose monk's robe brushed the floor as he shuffled along. As they walked down the corridor, lights flickered on to illuminate their path.

"You came just in time," the man explained. "We're having a town meeting." He took the last door to the right at the farthest end of the corridor, which led down yet another corridor. He paused before another rounded door. "We've been waiting for you to begin," he said. "We called a meeting as soon as we heard the commotion in the dunes. We've been waiting for you for a very, very long time."

The open doorway revealed a conclave of men and women in monkish robes, perhaps fifty of them, seated in a semicircle around an empty platform.

All of them turned toward the strangers who entered the room. The faces of the people gathered in the chamber were deeply wrinkled. Their hair came in several varieties of gray or white or silver. They were not merely old like Dody, but ancient. "Antediluvian," Dody muttered to himself, older than Noah's flood. It was a room full of Methuselahs.

As they walked, the people reached out to Dody with lean and spotted hands. The old man guided them to the platform, where Dody and Jonathan stood facing the crowd like Olympic champions. The audience of old ones rose to its feet and applauded, making a racket like a crowd at a basketball game.

"One of them is ersatz," someone shouted.

"But the other one's real," another voice responded.

"Has it really happened?" said a woman. "Has someone really come?"

"What do you think?" was the reply from Dody's guide.

The tumult rose and then subsided again.

Dody shyly asked, "Is Hoffman here?"

"He most certainly is," came the old man's reply. He grabbed Dody's hand and began pumping it up and down as if he were hoping to get water flowing up from a well again. "Hoffman is very pleased to meet you."

"Then you're the Great Hoffman?"

For the briefest of moments, Dody felt like weeping for this ancient person with a bowed body. But then he reminded himself that this was the Great Hoffman, the genius of a generation. A pioneer. A visionary. A living, breathing man of history.

"You'll help us, won't you?" Dody asked with such earnestness that there could be only one answer. "I know you can help us."

The old man straightened, lifting his great head from his chest. The face broadened as the mouth stretched across it. The gray-blue eyes looked out into the audience and beyond it. He was like a crumpled sail that had filled with air, like a flag unfurling in a steady breeze.

"The Great Hoffman," he said, more to himself than to Dody or Jonathan or the crowd of old ones. "The Great Hoffman will help you find your brother and your sister." He filled his chest with air and bellowed out his promise. "Of course, I will!"

"Well, I *was* the Great Hoffman," the old man replied thoughtfully, "when I was younger. Now, it's just plain old Hoffman, I'm afraid."

The crowd of old ones laughed.

Dody began pumping Hoffman's hand. If the arm had been a handle, it might have fallen from its socket. Overcome with joy, Jonathan rushed up to

Hoffman and hugged his brown, shapeless robe.

The crowd whispered and nodded. There was a smattering of applause. A cheer. And then quiet.

"We're so glad to find all of you!" Dody crowed, his voice cracking with emotion. "You'll know how to rescue Bobby and Elaine and help us get back to Earth."

"Rescue?" inquired Hoffman. He seemed shaken. "You want *me*, you want *us*, to help rescue *you*?" He made a strange muffled noise that sounded vaguely like a giggle and yet a little like a sob.

Dody was confused. "Why, yes, of course. That's why we came to you. We need your help."

The room fell silent.

"What's wrong?" Dody asked. Not a voice replied. "Is there anything the matter?" The silence settled in like a heavy fog, gloomy and impenetrable. "Can't you help rescue us?" He looked at one face after another. "Why do you all look so sad?"

Hoffman cleared his throat. "Uhummmmmm," he began. "It's just that we've been waiting for someone, for anyone, for almost thirty years." He paused long enough to catch a sob in his throat before it could escape. "Thirty years. Thirty long years of deprivation and isolation. Thirty years that saw our hopes dim like a dying candle. And now that you've come, you tell us that *you* need rescuing." He was able to continue only with great difficulty. "You see. We. Have been waiting. For you. To rescue. Us."

"Oh," said Dody. "Oh, I see. And I don't suppose

you know where we can find my brother, Bobby? Or how we can rescue my sister, Elaine?"

Hoffman had managed to stop crying but still appeared thoroughly mournful. "I'm afraid not, lad. I wouldn't know where to begin."

NINE
RESCUE

"OURS WAS THE FIRST SHIP to leave Earth," Hoffman began, as he, Dody and Jonathan were finishing
off a dinner of freeze-dried chicken *à la* king. The
sauce was white and sticky, as if someone had spilled
glue on the plate. Jonathan picked at the cubes of
rubbery meat, probably wishing he had something
green to eat. But for Dody, it was good to have real
food again, and he spooned up every bit.

"These are almost the last of our ship's stores,"
Hoffman said. "We've been saving them for a special
occasion such as this."

They sat in a small dining hall that was almost
identical to the galleys on board the *Wanderer*. Once
Dody had finished with his plate, Hoffman continued
the story of the first flight.

"We weren't sure that it would work," he said.
"The propulsion system had hardly been tested. We

planned to push our rockets to as close to the speed of light as we dared. You understand that the mass of an object increases as it nears light speed, and there was no telling whether or not the whole ship would fall to pieces as we accelerated.

"Well, we took the chance and everything went perfectly. Almost everything. But then you can't expect perfection in any human endeavor, which is why we sent so many ships to so many separate places. We wanted to be absolutely sure that some would survive.

"Every ship left off beacons along the way for others to follow. They were like marker buoys to guide the second wave of migration. Our flight went remarkably smoothly, until we arrived in orbit here. One by one, all four of our landing craft took off for the planet only to disappear, without the slightest trace. It was as if they'd been swallowed up whole, just the way yours was. Our commander wanted to return home. He was a competent man, but he had no vision. I, on the other hand, was fired with imagination.

"I proposed to land the spacecraft itself. I told the commander that there was nothing to it, that we would land safely, find the missing landers and return with their crews.

"He agreed, of course. How could he not? No one wanted to leave those men and women behind if there was a chance to rescue them. But instead of landing safely, the ship crashed into the planet like a cannonball. A horrible, horrible mess, of course. It was beyond repair. We'd designed the ship itself to withstand a considerable impact, but a quarter of the crew died when we plowed into the desert here."

Hoffman cleared his throat and rubbed an eye with the crook of a finger. But his eyes were dry, as if he had long ago used up all the tears allowed for a lifetime.

"Happily most of us, and almost all of the children, survived. It was a computer error that caused the disaster, as best we could determine, but we never knew with any certainty."

Dody interrupted him. "A little glitch," he said.

Hoffman glared at Dody, the way a teacher would stare at a student who had spoken without first raising his hand.

"As I was saying," the old man continued, "we salvaged what we could of the ship's stores. We made use of the hull, the generators, the tables and chairs, everything that we could. We built this place that you see, underground to protect us from the elements. The ship gave us everything we needed. There wasn't much water, though, even then. Even less now. We survive on what we can recycle and collect from the dew. An ingenious system really. I designed it myself.

"Those were very difficult days, I assure you. But we had plenty of food from our stores and seeds to grow if we managed our water very carefully. And there appeared to be no human disease organisms here, other than what we brought ourselves, so our health was surprisingly good. Surely few planets were as suited to human life as this. We lived on knowing that a second ship would eventually come if everything followed according to plan. And even if that failed, we would have established a colony here — a little outpost of Earth where humankind might survive.

"We had some good times. There was much music and the children acted out dramas and played their games. And we adults set about exploring the planet that was to be our home, most likely for the rest of our lives. All seemed well enough. But one day, when many of the adults were on an expedition to the sea, the Winnems came to our cave. You say you've seen them. They're more horse than man, strange wild beasts and all the more terrifying because they seemed at least partly human. They carried away the children. They even took away the last of our beacons, so that if a second ship did come, they would be hard-pressed to find us.

"That was a dark, dark day. You understand that I mean that figuratively, because the sun continued to shine. It rose and it set, but what joy there had been in our lives had been stripped away leaving us raw and angry.

"We organized a party of adults to rescue our sons and daughters. As you know, none of our ships carried arms or weapons of any kind. It was our hope, foolish hope you could say, that away from Earth we wouldn't need them. But the Winnems frightened us, so we fashioned weapons out of odds and ends that remained of the ship's wreckage. We searched out those creatures fully prepared to destroy them. I am afraid that we did not make the very best of soldiers. We were scientists and engineers, pilots and managers. Only a few of us had ever been trained for combat. Our equipment helped us succeed in finding the Winnems. They were not too far from here at a large oasis, a pond really, surrounded by tall, leafy plants, big as trees but more like giant ferns than anything else. We came upon the Winnems as they slept, standing on their feet in the shade in the middle of the day. Although they were larger and stronger than we were, they proved very easy to subdue. You see, they had never seen weapons before. After a few explosive rounds were fired they stopped stampeding about and froze in their tracks. It was as if they had turned to statues, ready to be carted off to the nearest museum. It was miraculous. But our children were nowhere to be found.

"One of our crew was a linguist. And I am something of an expert in languages myself. I speak seven fluently and can read an additional three — that's not counting English, of course. Be that as it may, the two of us were soon able to make sense of the strange whinnies and snorts that constituted the Winnem tongue. Smelly beasts the Winnems; they stink like a barnyard. Yet we found they were a simple people of some intelligence who had once ruled a planet of fruitful plains and bountiful forests. But they told us that a terrible monster had taken hold of their world and sucked it dry. Their people died in large numbers. And they had no choice but to do its bidding. They seemed to have no words to describe this creature or at least nothing that we could understand. They used a word that seemed to mean 'large,' but not on the same scale that we mean it. Large like the moons, they would say, but this hardly seemed likely.

" 'Errat' is what they called it. I still do not understand completely what they meant by it. Errat had demanded that they seize our children, they said. Yet at other times, they spoke of Errat as a place. Errat was where they were instructed to take the children. We demanded that the Winnems lead us there. And they seemed happy, even eager to help."

Hoffman stopped again to clear his throat. "Remember this, young man, if nothing else!" he said, shaking a finger at Dody, who did seem young in comparison to the old scientist. "Be watchful of the Winnems of this world. They'll let anyone become their masters!

"That was almost thirty Earth-years ago today, when the Winnems obediently led us to the greenish land that they called Errat. It was, as you know, a vast, barren place, and I despaired of ever finding the children again. Then they appeared out of no-where to greet us. We jumped for joy, we raced for them, we hugged them to our bosoms. But there was something not quite right about them. They looked healthy enough. They were neat and tidy. Cleaner, really, than any ordinary children ought to be, even our own. 'Where have you been?' we asked them. 'In the budding grove,' they answered. 'Were you treated kindly?' we asked. 'Never better,' they answered. The memory sends chills up and down my spine even now. They didn't seem like children at all.

"We were troubled but we took them home to our cave, hoping, I suppose, that their strange man-ner and appearance might be the result of their being forcibly taken from us. Yet it was not long before many of us began to feel that these were not our children at all — not ours or anybody else's."

At first, Hoffman had spoken in a spirited, almost jovial manner, as if he were discussing an exciting new book he had read or a scientific discovery. But then suddenly his mood and tempo changed, the way an orchestra does when it reaches a symphony's slow movement. His face became solemn and he pulled a kerchief from somewhere within his mo-nastic robe and dabbed at the corner of an eye as if a piece of grit were lodged there. He placed his head close to Dody's, so close that Dody could smell the dinner on Hoffman's breath, a hint of garlic and onion from the chicken à la king.

"My wife, Miriam, and I had a child, too. A boy.

David was his name. Dave or Davey we called him. When he came back to us from Errat he was utterly transformed. He was perfectly obedient. He went to sleep without fussing and ate every last bite at dinner without a complaint. It was as if he were a machine designed to please us and not a proper boy at all. Needless to say, Miriam and I became quite upset. 'Davey just isn't himself since he came back,' Miriam said. 'If he isn't himself, then who is he?' I wanted to know, but I knew exactly what she meant. In short, he wasn't our boy. He had no fight, no gumption. Then one day we noticed that instead of growing, he had begun to shrivel a bit. It was Miriam who noticed the hump."

Dody interrupted. "He was sporing. Like Walter."

"That's what Davey told us, as if it were the most natural thing in the world. He said, 'I'm just sporing, Dad,' as if it happened all the time. We thought that a horrible disease had attacked our boy, a plague that might infect the other children and in the end might destroy all of us. But we couldn't throw our own little Davey out into the desert. On the other hand, he didn't seem to be our own little Davey. He continued shriveling, and the hump continued growing. It was an awful thing to behold. He was my own son, but a more grotesque being I had never seen in my life."

"Just like Walter," Dody said, as much to himself as the others.

"I talked to the others," Hoffman continued.

"They thought he might have a strange disease. We put him into isolation, in a room with a large window where we took turns keeping an eye on him. It was horrible to see it happen. The large lump growing on his back seemed to be draining the life from his body. He was shriveling and cracking before our eyes. And then something we had not imagined possible occurred. He exploded one day, in a puff, filling the room with a dark dust that slowly settled on the floor. Miriam wanted to go in to see what had happened to Dave, but we wouldn't let her. I had to bar the door to keep her out, if you can imagine it. For days we stood watch. The floor of the room where Davey had been seemed suddenly to come alive. Out of the dust grew small, writhing creatures, like spidery starfish, but with only four arms. There were millions of them.

"We took no chances," the old man continued. "We incinerated everything in the room. Miriam and I were shattered, of course. Our son was gone. We would never see him again. But it didn't stop with Davey. One of the engineer's daughters began to shrivel just as our boy had. A pretty little girl, until it began.

"We had no choice, you'll agree. We couldn't destroy them, but we couldn't keep them, either. If they *were* our children, they had been changed into something different. Or perhaps they were some other kind of creature that only looked and acted like they were ours. Whatever the truth, we turned them out, all of them. It eased our consciences to know that they still can be seen roaming about Errat, no different from the way they looked so many years ago. That proves that we were right, you see. They are young still, these creatures that seem to be our children. It's as if they are fixed in time forever, and all the while we ourselves are growing older and older, as you can see, old and ready to die. To lose our children was a terrible thing, and we were disheartened. No more children were ever born to us here, and for many there seemed nothing more to live for.

"Miriam wandered away one day, all alone out into the desert. We never found a trace. There were a large number who left us in that way, I'm afraid. We searched the desert for them, but not a strip of clothes, not a skeleton could we find."

"Those silvery insects!" Dody blurted out.

"Scourers," Jonathan said.

Hoffman was confused by the interruption. He closed his eyes to remember where he had left off. "Those of us who stayed here in our cave have been waiting patiently these many years, hoping for rescue before the last remnants of humanity vanish from this planet. And without a beacon to guide you to us, we had slim hope of anyone discovering us.

"Your friend is the first of his kind to be permitted to enter here since we expelled the children. He's welcome, because he's your friend. But let me assure you, he bears watching."

"He's really a very nice boy, once you get to know him," Dody said. "He helped me try to stop the Winnems from taking Elaine."

"You don't seem to realize that his is a rival species," Hoffman said. "However 'nice' he seems to be, his kind is in competition with our own. They've beaten back the Winnems, and they'll beat us back, too, if we're not careful. It's like flies and spiders. And in this case, we're the flies, and *they* are the spiders. They don't care one whit about what might become of *us*."

"That's not true," Jonathan said. "I care a lot about what happens to Elaine and Dody. They're my friends."

"Even now, I doubt your sincerity," Hoffman said bitterly.

"Put me to the test, Dody," said Jonathan. "Let me show you that I can rescue Elaine from the Winnems."

"And how do you propose to do that?" Hoffman asked.

Jonathan had no reply to that.

"We'll do just what you did," Dody said. "We'll attack their oasis by day and frighten them into giving up Elaine. And then we'll force them to help us find Bobby for us."

Dody was very excited. The three Ramsey children would be reunited, and they would owe it all to him and to Jonathan.

"I'm afraid I'm too old and feeble to frighten anyone," Hoffman said.

"But won't you help Jonathan and me find the oasis?" Dody asked.

"I suppose I could. I'm not as quick on my feet as I once was, you understand. But I might be able to lead you there," Hoffman said. "You'll have to carry the water for all of us."

"How soon can we leave?" Dody asked.

"We can't go tonight. From your experience, that would appear to be too dangerous. Best to wait until morning, after we've all had a good sleep."

Dody and Jonathan followed the old man as he led them to their sleeping quarters, a room almost identical to the one that Dody had slept in on the *Wanderer*.

Later, Dody found he could not sleep at all. He lay in his berth, sandwiched between Jonathan, silent in the berth above him, and Hoffman, turning and snorting in the bunk below. The nights were long on planet 5, and this one seemed to wear on interminably. "Davey," he heard the old one mumble in his sleep. "Miriam, wake up the boy! He'll be late for school!"

By morning Dody was thoroughly exhausted. But he had worked out the details of the rescue mission. Hoffman would lead them to the oasis. But the rest would be up to Dody and Jonathan. They would fashion weapons that they could use to frighten the Winnems, not to harm them, just as Hoffman had done thirty years before.

Dody hardly touched his breakfast of scrambled eggs and bacon. The fat tasted faintly rancid. Perhaps even freeze-dried food spoiled after more than a century. Or it might have been that his stomach was churning with the thought of encountering the Winnems again, even by day when they were said to be in such a placid state.

Neither he nor Jonathan said more than a grunt or two during the meal. However, the Great Hoffman seemed to come alive at the thought of an attack and rescue.

"It's got my juices flowing again," he said. "We retrieve Elaine and find Bobby. With your help, perhaps I can rig up a transmitter to contact your parents. They'll take us all back to Earth with them.

"We hibernate, of course, and wake up no worse for wear in the year 8125, if my calculations are correct.

"We're settling the fate of the universe, you know. We can warn everyone about the dangers here. With the right equipment, we can eradicate Errat and make this planet habitable for others.

"It's quite simple, really," Hoffman said.

Everything was simple for Hoffman, Dody thought. But then Hoffman didn't have to face the Winnems again.

"On Earth, naturally, we'll be hailed as heroes. That is, whoever is left after all these thousands of years will surely hail us. If they have records, that is. If they have histories. And with the information that we've gathered, we'll go back out again and settle this planet and many others.

"We'll take a few million people with us the next time so that we can really move in. We've got to begin now, before the sun's core collapses and a shell of hot gas encompasses the earth." Hoffman was breathless. "We can't get started soon enough."

"I'll be happy if we can just find my brother and sister and then get us all back to my parents," Dody said.

"But you've got to see the larger picture," Hoffman said. "I've had plenty of time to think about things. I've even thought of placing myself in hibernation for a few centuries to see what happens to our species. I want to wake up to new worlds full of vast cities of busy, healthy people. I want to see my vision fulfilled."

The speech left him a little winded.

Dody had had plenty of time to think, too. And he understood that in any complicated plan, many things could go wrong. There would be mistakes made, miscalculations, glitches. The fate of humankind, like the fate of the universe, could not be totally predicted. It would be better, he thought, to take one small step at a time.

"Shouldn't we get ready for the Winnems?" Dody asked, while Hoffman was still catching his breath.

"Quite right, quite right," Hoffman replied.

With the help of the other old ones, Dody gathered and packed the weapons and supplies they would need. The old people, many of them in their seventies and eighties — all of them older than

Dody — worked slowly and tenatively, as if fearful they would drop and break something if they moved too fast. Dody felt he and Jonathan could do the job more quickly themselves. But he knew that this was a ritual of leave-taking and that everyone, even the most tired and enfeebled, needed to play a part.

When all was ready, they walked to the giant portal, which Hoffman unlocked with great ceremony. Several of the men and women helped him pull the door all the way open. A cascade of sand swept over their feet. The brilliant light was briefly blinding.

"Do not despair that I am leaving you," Hoffman said. "You must wait patiently and pray for our success."

The old ones helped strap packs on the backs of the three adventurers. Hoffman's was by far the lightest of the three, filled mostly with loaves of bread made of a coarse, synthetic flour.

Two women presented Jonathan and Dody with huge water jugs supported by slings to carry them into the desert.

"Take our water," said one of the women, "that you may return to us again."

And then one by one, the assembled old ones hugged the travelers. There were no tears, but no smiles either, only a determined, mournful silence.

"We're off to save the universe for humankind," Hoffman said, "whatever the cost to us might be." He stood tall and straight, and did his best to show no sign of concern that he might never see his friends again.

But when the old ones closed the large, round door, Dody did not feel heroic.

Already, early in the day, the desert air was scalding. In the distance, Dody could see mirages — the illusion of pools of water, shimmering in the sun.

They walked slowly and steadily, pausing often to sip from their water jugs. "There's no sense saving it," Dody said, remembering the advice his father used to give him on backpacking trips. "What we don't drink we have to carry."

Finally Hoffman led them up to the crest of an enormous dune, hundreds of feet high. There below them, in a valley between two dunes, was the unlikely sight of a lush oasis, a patch of cool green surrounded by hot, red sand.

"Are the Winnems down there?" Dody whispered.

"Look carefully and you'll see a few of them, sleeping on their feet by the edge of the oasis."

They were standing stock-still under giant ferns. "How many are there?" Dody asked.

"Thirty years ago, there might have been ten thousand here. But climatic changes have reduced their numbers," Hoffman said. "I'd say there are no more than two thousand."

"Two *thousand*?" Dody asked.

"I'm being generous, of course," Hoffman said. "Theirs is a dying race."

"The two of us are supposed to scare two thousand of them?"

"It was *your* idea," said the older man. "I would have advised against it. By Jupiter! If I were younger, I'd go with you," Hoffman said. "But things being what they are, you youngsters will have to handle it without me."

"Let's go, Jonathan," Dody said. "Elaine may be down there. We need to find her."

Jonathan was still smiling. "I'll go first if you want me to," he said.

"We'll go together," Dody said.

They divided their few weapons between them. In fact, these were scarcely weapons at all, but large noisemakers and fireworks, contrived by Dody to frighten but not to harm. For the first time in his life, Dody wished he had a real weapon. Even a very sharp sword would do. A Winnem might weigh two hundred fifty pounds, perhaps even more, and they were tough, sinewy creatures with heavy haunches and hooves as big as a plow horse's. Their bodies were weapons, Dody thought, quite capable of kicking or trampling a human to death.

Still, there was no use thinking about the possible danger any longer. The day was only growing warmer.

Hoffman reached for Dody's hand and shook it with great excitement. "Show them your grit, lad," he said. And then he turned to Jonathan and shook his hand as well. "I'm beginning to think I've been wrong about you, laddy," he said.

"Let's go," Dody said.

The two began moving down the hill of sand, first walking, then racing. Dody let out a bellow, an apelike roar that would have made a gorilla blanch and tremble. They ran and slid and sometimes stumbled down, yelling all the way. But the oasis answered them only with an unnatural calm and quiet. They passed a few Winnems who appeared to be asleep on their feet just as Hoffman had said. They did not seem to notice Jonathan and Dody, who yelled and rattled their weapons as they swept by.

Into the ferny trees the two of them ran, through arches of branch and leaf, into a cool shade that deepened as they neared the pool at the center of the oasis.

They had seen a dozen Winnems, no more, all seemingly frozen into place. They fired their weapons, with bangs and an outpouring of smoke as great as from any blunderbuss.

But there was no general stampede. The few Winnems had slipped quietly away and, except for Dody and Jonathan, there was no sign of life left in the oasis. It was as if the Winnems knew they were coming and had a secret battle plan of their own.

"Looking for somebody, Dody?"

The voice came from the green fronds that hung over them and then a creature dropped down beside them.

"Bobby!" Dody threw himself at his big brother, wrapped him in his arms and the two of them fell clumsily to the ground. Dody wondered again whether he'd cracked a rib, but he didn't care if he had. "Bobby!" he shouted again.

"Who'd you expect?" It was another voice from the trees. A vine dropped from the branch, and Elaine slid down it.

"Dody," she said. "I was worried about you." When he got to his feet, she rushed up and hugged him.

And then she hugged Jonathan as well. "You were so brave when the Winnems came after me," she said. "I was worried about both of you."

"Well, now that we've rescued you, you don't have to worry," Dody said.

"Rescued?" Elaine began to laugh. "Me?"

"From the Winnems!" Dody said.

Just then, the ground under their feet began to shake. The air filled with the sounds of cattle on the run and then their smell. Wild-eyed, the awakened Winnems galloped toward them.

But instead of trampling them directly, the beasts made a wide circle about them and then stopped. They were quiet except for their puffing and snorting.

"Don't worry," Dody said, ready to fire off one of the explosive tubes he was carrying. "We'll frighten them off. We won't let them hurt you!"

"Those big, furry puppies?" Elaine laughed again. "They wouldn't have hurt me for anything, or anybody else who's a friend of Bobby's."

"They'll do whatever I ask," Bobby said.

"He's become a kind of king around here," Elaine explained. "He sent them out looking for us, you know. But they got confused when they found three of us instead of two." She lowered her voice. "The Winnems are not very bright," she said. "But they're kind and generous. And now we're all together again."

"Don't you want to introduce me to your friend?" Bobby asked. "You must be Jonathan," he said as he shook the boy's hand. "You know, you look an awful lot like the guys who chased after me when I got out of the lander. If I hadn't been able to outrun them, I don't know what would have happened."

"It might have been awful," Elaine said. "But this one's our friend."

"Now all we have to do is find a way to get back to the spaceship," Dody said.

"I was just getting to like it down here," Bobby said.

"Mom and Dad must be worried sick," Elaine reminded him.

"Yeah," Bobby said. "But even if we wanted to, how do we let them know where to find us?"

"Dody will think of something," Elaine said.

"I know a way to get back to your spaceship," Jonathan said.

"You do?" said Dody.

"We just have to find the landing craft."

"But it's been swallowed up and lost forever."

"Swallowed up, but not lost forever," Jonathan said. "I'll help you find it."

"Does that mean going back to those tunnels?" Elaine asked.

"I'm afraid it does," Jonathan said. "But I don't think the others will catch us."

"But what if they do?" Elaine said. "What'll happen to us if they do?"

"You'll be copied," Jonathan said.

TEN
FLIGHT

THE WINNEMS DID SMELL like a barnyard, like horses
and cows, like haystacks and manure piles, like sweat
and dust. Dody rode piggyback on one of them, his
legs sticking straight out and his arms clutching for
a hold around the Winnem's neck, all the while
getting a good whiff of the Winnem scent. He remembered the Missouri farm where his great-uncle
lived amid horses, chickens and one brindled cow
with brown, lonesome eyes. Dody liked the smell,
but Elaine did not. She conspicuously pinched her
nostrils shut with one hand and held on for dear life
with the other, as she raced toward Errat on the
back of a galloping Winnem of her own. "The stink!"
she shouted to Dody. "I think I'm going to be sick."
But to Dody, the Winnem smell was a remembrance
of life past, when he was young and his days shone
bright.

Bobby was ahead of the rest, astride the largest Winnem in the herd, a brute with great muscular shoulders and shining hair the color of a burnt umber crayon. "Yahooooo!" Bobby yelled, encouraging his Winnem to charge ahead even faster than the others. The Winnems proved to be strong, sure-footed creatures with seemingly limitless endurance as they galloped up the dunes in the lingering twilight of planet 5. Their footing was less certain on the steep, spongy slopes of Errat itself, where they slowed to an amble while climbing the barren, green terrain.

Hoffman had joined the Ramsey children after he saw from a distance that there was to be no battle after all. Now he, too, clung to the back of a Winnem in a journey that had jarred his every joint and bone. He was grateful for the sudden easing of the pace, but he was ready to stretch his worn-out body on the Errat ground, which was as soft as a mattress. "Are we almost there?" he asked. "Can't we stop awhile?"

"Stop, up ahead!" hollered Jonathan. His light, almost weightless body was perched upon a Winnem's sinewy shoulders, high above all the others.

In response, Bobby let out a long, high-pitched whinny, and all the Winnems fell into tight formation about him and halted.

"Dismount, ho!" Bobby commanded, but his companions had already jumped from their strange steeds.

With his scissors, Jonathan once again opened up

a slit in the surface of Errat, and he and the others gorged themselves with the pulpy fruit and bubbly fluid. But the Winnems would not partake. They whinnied and snorted to one another as if complaining that there was nothing here that could slake their thirst or satisfy their hunger.

"Thanks to Errat, giver of life," Jonathan said.

"Delicious!" Bobby declared.

"Errat is bountiful," Jonathan said, as if completing a prayer. "Errat leads us home."

"Very refreshing indeed," Hoffman said. "Like nectar and ambrosia, it rejuvenates body and spirit."

"How do we get to the lander?" Dody asked. He felt as if the others were so caught up in their adventure that they had forgotten why they had come. *He* was the practical one. *He* would get them to the *Wanderer*.

"What's the hurry?" Bobby demanded. "Aren't we having a terrific time?"

"I've had enough adventure to last a lifetime," Elaine said. "Now I just want to get back to Mom and Dad."

Dody could see that she was about to cry, and he placed his arm lightly over her shoulders. "I'll get us home," Dody promised her. He was surprised by his own resolve. He did not think he could bear it if she started sobbing. If she did, he, too, would certainly begin bawling, and he didn't want that. They had to get off this planet. He thought of the teeth that Jonathan had shown him. How many more teeth must there be from all the children who had been copied in the budding grove?

Dody was sure they were in mortal danger here, even though their bellies were full, and even though Jonathan was leading them to the landing craft. And the danger they were running from was not just to them, but to their parents, to the crew of the *Wanderer*, and to all those who remained behind on Earth.

"Here's the entrance," Jonathan said.

There it was, a round hole that might have been made by a giant rabbit. Or was it a pore in the surface of Errat? Or a mouth for swallowing them up?

"Let's go," Dody said. As frightened as he was, he was eager to do something about their plight instead of just worrying about it.

"Mount up!" said Bobby, but the Winnems backed away. He whinnied and snorted at them, and they whinnied and snorted back.

"They're not much interested," Bobby said.

"They say it's entirely too dangerous to go on," Hoffman explained more fully. "I'm afraid they're in revolt."

"I don't blame them," Elaine said. "It's disgusting down there. Couldn't some of us stay up here and wait for the others?"

"Let's not get separated again," Dody pleaded.

"All for one and one for all!" Bobby said. The Winnems snorted at him, whinnied and then charged across the Errat plain, back toward the desert.

"A bunch of chickens," Bobby complained. "But we're on our own at last," he said, brightening. "Let's get moving. Jonathan, lead the way. Lander, ho!"

The boy obediently dropped into the opening and the others followed — Bobby, Elaine and Dody, and then Hoffman, slower than the rest, taking care not to break any bones.

The tunnel felt even moister and mustier than it had before their journey into the desert. The faint light that glowed from the walls left no shadows. The travelers slipped frequently as if walking on ice, while nimble Jonathan led them down into a maze of corridors. The boy stopped often to let Dody and the old scientist catch up with the others, only to plunge far ahead again.

"This way, this way," he said excitedly. "Not much further. Almost there."

He had been saying it for more than an hour, for long enough that the others no longer believed him.

"Let's stop for a spell," Hoffman said, dropping to the ground and refusing to go any further. They all stopped.

Dody wasn't sure whether he was the first to notice a peculiar sound, a dull rhythm that was felt more than heard. It was like the beat of kettledrums in a Beethoven symphony.

"The roll of distant drums," Bobby declared. "Enemy tribes in hot pursuit."

"Piffle," said Hoffman, who sat massaging his calf muscles. "It's nothing of the kind."

"What is it then?" Elaine asked.

The sound was gradually growing louder.

"Feet," Dody said, unsure of how he knew. "Hundreds of feet."

"Thousands," Jonathan explained. "In the tunnels, chasing after us."

"What'd I tell you?" said Bobby.

"What'll they do if they catch us?" Elaine demanded.

"They'll take us to the budding grove," Dody said.

"And copy us!" Elaine added.

"I knew it!" Hoffman said, jumping up to his feet. He was for a brief moment jublilant to know that he had been right for thirty years. "Perfect copies. Children who look like our children but aren't our children — who aren't children at all! They're ersatz. Phony. Fraudulent. I knew it all along!"

"What're you talking about?" Bobby asked.

"They can make an exact duplicate of you," Elaine said.

"That'd be great," Bobby said. "I could be a twin. Or a triplet, even. Terrific."

"It's not like that," Elaine explained. "There'd be nothing left of you, except your teeth. You'd be dead."

"Deader than a doornail," Jonathan said.

"My little Davey," Hoffman said. "My poor boy. That creature who came home to Miriam and me so many years ago was not our little Davey at all. Just a copy. I knew it! He looked like Davey, but you can't fool a mother or a father, not for long." He was crying as if his son had been gone for just a day or two and not for decades. "Forgive an old man," he said. "I don't know why I'm carrying on like this. We lost him so very long ago."

The pulsing sound of running feet was getting louder, the danger nearer, with every step.

"We should go," Jonathan said, "or they'll catch you."

"Move along, then, move along," Hoffman said as the sound of feet hitting spongy ground made the tunnel shake.

"This way!" Jonathan said.

Dody and the others sped after him. They were running for their lives.

"He's a good lad, this one," Hoffman said. He puffed as he trotted along, trying to keep up with the others. "Not at all like the others. Wants to help us. Still I wonder where he's taking us."

The rumbling beat of running feet was getting even louder.

The five of them ran until Hoffman and Dody could run no longer. The others slowed for them, jogging instead of running. Then they walked instead of jogging.

Dody was winded. His lungs felt as if there were embers burning deep inside them. If he had to run any more, he was sure his chest would burst into flame. Back at home, he'd been able to run on and on, to race his friends across a field or through the park. Now, unable to catch a breath, he felt as if he were about to collapse like a hot air balloon with a rip in its fabric.

Dody knew that the Errat children never tired. The rhythm of their running feet rolled on, louder and louder.

Jonathan begged them all to start running again, but Dody could hardly lift his feet, and Hoffman could barely shuffle forward.

"You shouldn't wait for me," Hoffman said. "Press on, press on."

But they all waited.

"It's not much farther," Jonathan promised, moving ahead of the others again.

"You've been saying that for hours!" Elaine said in a burst of anger.

"It's just down this way," Jonathan said, turning down another corridor, now running as he cried, "We're here! We're here!"

Suddenly energized, even Hoffman and Dody found the strength to run after him.

They soon caught up with Jonathan, who had reached a place where the tunnel stopped. A fleshy wall blocked their progress.

"It's a dead end," Bobby said. "Jonathan's tricked us. We're doomed."

Jonathan was hurt by the accusation. "You're my friends," he said. "I'd never trick you. This is it! The lander's just on the other side of this wall. But we've got to be careful. It could be guarded."

"I knew it!" Bobby said. "We should have brought those weapons."

"They wouldn't have done much good," Jonathan assured him. He pushed against the wall. It opened into a huge cave, the biggest that the Ramsey children had seen. The walls glowed with a hazy light. And in the middle, filling most of the chamber, sat the lander, its surfaces still gleaming.

"Wow!" said Bobby. "It looks as good as new. How'd it get here, anyway? It couldn't have come through that door."

"Errat brought it here," Jonathan explained.

"Did he take it apart first?" Bobby said. "It's like a ship in a bottle."

"Errat swallowed it whole," Dody said, remembering the way it had disappeared into a crater soon after they landed.

Hoffman nodded. "Most likely, Errat surrounded it the way the skin does a splinter or any foreign body that intrudes upon it. That must be the way that all our landing craft vanished without a trace. Isn't that so, Jonathan lad?"

"Something like that," Jonathan agreed.

"But how do we get it out of here?" Bobby asked.

"I'm not sure," Jonathan said. "But there has to be a way."

Suddenly a hum came from the landing craft, followed by a low rumble of turning wheels and gears. A plate of metal dropped down slowly from the lander's sleek underside.

The platform had a single passenger, a little withered man with a huge hump on his back.

"Who's the funny little guy?" Bobby asked.

"That's Walter," Elaine said.

Bobby moved toward the scurrying little man to get a better look.

"I wouldn't touch him," Elaine said.

"Why not?" Bobby asked.

"No touching!" Walter pleaded.

But as the clumsy little man tried to back away, almost in reflex, Bobby reached after him, grabbing him by the collar.

"No touching!" Walter screamed.

Bobby certainly had not meant to hurt him. But that single, unthinking touch was enough.

Walter disappeared in a puff of spores. Without a sound, he'd exploded into a cloud of what looked like smoke — a vile-smelling swirl of spores that enveloped all of them.

And all the while the rhythmic beat of running feet was drawing even closer, rocking the cavern with the force of a small earthquake.

"Quick! Into the lander!" Dody ordered them.

Only Jonathan raced with him through the fog of spores and onto the platform. The others limped ahead, too stunned to move very quickly.

Just as they all climbed up onto the platform, the flap of wall opened up behind them and a stream of Errat children began flowing into the cave. Their numbers seemed unending, like an invasion of ants. Even through the haze of spores, Dody recognized some of the children who had captured him and Elaine when they first landed. He spotted a little redheaded boy, a taller one with jet-black ringlets and a girl with beautiful golden hair.

The children had packed into the cave, thousands of them, surrounding the landing craft. All at once, they drew their wooden swords from their scabbards.

The pounding rhythm of running children had ended, and Dody could hear the whistle and wheeze of Hoffman's breathing beside him.

Dody realized that if he did not act quickly, he and the others would be taken prisoner easily, no matter how hard they fought. They would be caught and copied. They would be "dead as doornails," just as Jonathan had said. But their parents wouldn't know that, not at first. They would think that the copies were real, and would take them back to Earth. What the danger would be, Dody was not entirely sure, but he knew he would fight to the last if necessary to avoid being copied and reduced to a handful of teeth.

Dody did all that thinking in the smallest fraction of a second. Then he leaped toward the computer terminal on the platform, and as soon as he was able to type out instructions, he and his companions began to rise slowly into the landing craft.

"Stop them!" shouted the girl with golden hair. "Don't let them get away!"

The children swarmed toward the rising platform, screaming and shouting. "Get them! Grab them!"

Dody did his best to push the copy children away, and the others helped him, especially Hoffman, who seemed rejuvenated by the fight.

"Hold them back!" Hoffman shouted.

"Clobber them!" Bobby yelled.

But Dody saw that the children's army was far too large to fight off. It would soon overrun the landing craft, no matter how hard he and the others struggled. Still, Dody did his best to toss one light little body after another back into the sea of ersatz children below the lander. Bobby and Elaine seemed to be having a fine time, pushing back their enemies, who climbed over one another in order to reach the rising platform. They were clambering on board even faster than they could be thrown back.

Soon, Dody and the others were being steadily pummeled by blows from hundreds of wooden swords, which battered them to the ground. One of the children must have reached the computer terminal, because instead of rising, the platform now began to descend.

"Don't give up!" Dody said, but his voice was no more than a hoarse whisper, a signal less of courage than of certain defeat. The platform stopped. Soon he felt dozens of hands pulling at him and lifting him into the air.

"To the budding grove!" someone shouted.

"To the budding grove!" came the response from hundreds of voices in dreadful unison.

But before the many hands could carry Dody and the others away, a solitary voice cried out above all the rest.

"Halt!" it said.

The order had an immediate effect on the Errat children. They froze in their places and waited in silence.

"Put them down," said the same commanding voice, more softly now. It was Jonathan.

Dody and Hoffman, Elaine and Bobby, were all put back on their feet, like bowling pins that had been picked up and righted.

All around them the thousands of children who had packed into the chamber knelt down, their heads on the ground, their arms thrust forward.

"Arise, children of Errat," Jonathan said. "These are not your enemies. Leave us alone."

He was calm and smiling as the ersatz children obeyed his every order, rising to their feet and moving noiselessly away through open flaps in the chamber's walls.

"Hooray for Jonathan!" Elaine shouted as she threw her arms around his neck.

"How'd you do that?" Bobby asked.

"It was easy," Jonathan explained. "They're used to obeying orders. But I think we'd better leave as quickly as we can. Before they stop to change their minds."

Dody typed instructions into the terminal.

With a hiss like the door of a school bus, the platform finally joined the floor of the lander, shutting tight. "They can't touch us now," Bobby said.

Dody should have felt safe, but he didn't. They had recovered the landing craft and were safely inside it, but he wasn't sure what he was supposed to do next. How were they going to get it out of the cave? He turned to Jonathan.

"Is there a way out of here?" Dody asked the boy, certain that he would help them if he could.

"I thought you could figure that out," the boy said, no longer smiling in his usual carefree way.

Suddenly, after only a slight hesitation, Dody knew exactly what needed to be done. "Prepare for takeoff," he commanded the others.

He began pushing buttons and flipping switches, each step in the sequence signaled by a series of green lights on the control panel.

The viewing screen came to life, showing the glistening, fleshlike ceiling above them. There was no way out, Dody thought, but he followed the bidding of the computer, punching at the panel and lighting it up as if he were decorating it for Christmas.

"Prepare for launch," said Mickey's familiar, calming voice. Was there a trace of a scowl in it this time, Dody wondered? A hint that their prospects were doubtful, at best? After all, how could they take off from a cave?

They all took their places in reclining chairs.

Everyone looked a bit nervous, except Hoffman, who was smiling in his eagerness to begin a new adventure.

"There's an obstruction overhead," Mickey noted without undue alarm. "I recommend that you abort takeoff."

Dody responded by pushing a series of buttons on the control panel.

"Do you truly want to override my recommendation?" Mickey asked.

In reply, Dody pressed other buttons and flipped other switches.

"Very well," Mickey said. "I'll begin the countdown. Ten seconds to launch."

A roar of engines filled the cavern, making it difficult to hear the count, but occasional numbers rose above the din. "Eight." "Five." "Two." "One." "Launch underway." The craft lurched upward.

Then the howling began. A cry of torment and of pain, even louder than the engines, a sound that seemed to come from everywhere, from deep within the tunnels and flesh of Errat itself.

"What is that?" Bobby shouted as loudly as he could.

"Were there any children left in the cave?" asked Elaine, shouting to make herself heard above the blast of engines and the animal scream.

"They're safe and sound," Jonathan said. "It's the cry of Errat herself."

"Is it — is she — hurt?" Elaine asked.

163

Jonathan himself seemed wounded. He was still not smiling. "It's the heat of the engines," he said. "It causes Errat a lot of pain."

The screen above them suddenly showed a flash of moon and stars as the roof of the cave opened up like a mouth. Dody realized that the lander was making its own escape route as it rose, ripping through the very flesh of Errat.

"Liftoff plus ten," Mickey said.

The speed of ascent quickened, pressing the lander's passengers into their chairs. As the craft emerged from the cavern, the screen showed the moonlit surface of Errat, falling away behind them. Where the lander had been only seconds before, a jagged wound broke the dimly lighted plain.

"We're safe," Dody declared. "I was afraid we were going to burn up from our own heat."

"Hurrah, hurray!" shouted Hoffman. "I never thought I'd ever get away."

"Me, neither," Elaine confessed.

"What was there to worry about?" Bobby said, all of his own worries already forgotten.

"I'm not sure we're safe yet," Jonathan said. "Look." He pointed to the screen.

There above them they could see the giant X, its four arms clasping planet 5 as the globe slowly turned into the light of a new day.

The X seemed to twitch.

"It's alive," Bobby said.

"Of course, it's alive," Elaine said. "I'm glad we got away in time."

"We may not be in time," Jonathan said. "Errat can be swift when she's angry."

As he spoke, one of the arms of the X moved, almost imperceptibly at first and then swiftly and surely. The giant arm — a huge tentacle that could reach across a continent — loosened its grip, lifted up and reached for their landing craft. It tried to swat the offending object the way a man might swipe at a mosquito that had bitten him on the elbow. The arm of Errat was long and powerful.

"Oh, my," Dody said. "Oh, my oh, my."

The tentacle stretched out through the atmosphere of planet 5 and reached into the coldness of empty space.

It was moving toward them, faster than the landing craft could speed away.

But then the entire planet began to wobble, like a top losing its spin. And in an instant, it flew out of its orbit and off the screen.

"Boy, that was close!" Bobby said.

" 'Bye, 'bye, Errat," said Elaine, glad to be rid of it.

"My old friends, all gone," Hoffman said, sobbing. There was no hope that anyone on the planet could have survived.

"And your friends, too," Dody said to Jonathan.

If Jonathan was upset, he did not show it. "I'm with my friends," he said cheerily. "And we're on our way home."

ELEVEN
SLEEPERS, WAKE!

THE RAMSEY CHILDREN and their friends could see the *Wanderer* magnified on the lander's viewing screen. Through the craft's portholes, the huge spaceship still looked tiny in the distance, like a model hanging by invisible strings against a black backdrop.

They were just minutes from their rendezvous now, and they should have been jubilant. But a gloom had settled in like a spell of bad weather, because Dody could not make contact with the mother ship.

"No radio, no radio," Dody repeated to himself.

"What can we do, Dody?" asked Elaine, who looked small and pale and very queasy from being weightless.

"Nothing to do but land her," Dody said.

They were closing in on the *Wanderer* now. It was so near that they could have leaped across the little gap that separated the two craft. As much as the Ramsey children wanted to see their parents immediately, they did not dare go aboard until the lander was thoroughly cleaned.

Dody insisted on it.

"Look at all the dust we've tracked along with us," he said, sounding like one of his own parents. "We've got to vacuum up every spore."

"Do we have to?" Bobby asked.

"If we miss just one and it gets into the *Wanderer*, it'd be a disaster," Dody said.

Hoffman agreed. "From such little seeds as these, came that monstrous tentacled thing, Errat," he said. He was sprawled out on a chair, too tired out to help with the cleanup. "A single spore could grow up to such proportions and suck the Earth dry as it did planet 5."

"We don't have any choice if we want to see Mom and Dad again," Dody said.

But as they all plunged into the job, he worried about the radio silence. He could not help wondering whether they would ever see their parents again or if something on board the *Wanderer* had gone terribly wrong.

The work of cleaning up was difficult, because an individual spore was smaller than a poppy seed, and there were millions of them.

"Little bits of Walter!" Elaine complained. "It's so disgusting!"

As they worked, they discovered that it was difficult to move around the crew's compartment without stirring up a thin cloud of spores. They donned masks to keep from inhaling the dust. They vacuumed everything, sweeping through all the corners and crevices. It was housekeeping, but it had to be done with painstaking thoroughness, again and again and again, and so it proved worse than any chores the Ramsey children had ever had to do back on Earth.

"This is very boring," Bobby said.

"Better than waking up with a baby Errat around your neck," Elaine said. "Please hurry. I want to see Mom and Dad right away."

There was a lot to do. All the soiled coveralls had to be incinerated; the landing craft's furniture jettisoned into space; the carpeting peeled up from the deck and destroyed. Only a sanitized shell would remain when the lander returned to the main spacecraft.

Jonathan pitched in, happily doing whatever Dody asked.

As they all worked at their tasks, Dody hummed a tune from Bach, the piece he liked to play on the *Wanderer*'s organ. "Sleepers, Wake!" it was called. Surely there was no more beautiful music ever written. But Dody was never very good at holding to a single key. And when he hummed, the tone was high-pitched and nasal — more a drone than a melody.

"Quit it," Bobby snapped.

"Quit what?" Dody responded, not sure what he had done to antagonize his brother.

"Can the humming, Dody," Bobby said.

"Was I humming? I didn't realize," Dody said. "Of course, I'll stop if it bothers you."

"I liked it," Jonathan said.

"Who asked you?" said Bobby sharply.

"Nobody asked me," said the other boy. "But I like it when Dody hums. He promised he'd play the organ for me when we go aboard the *Wanderer*. I've never heard music before, and I like it."

"You've got to be kidding," Bobby said. "It's just like Professor Hoffman told us. You can't be human!"

"Now, now, lad," the old man said. "I've spoken rashly at times, I know. The boy is human enough, and he's proven a real friend to us all."

"I did like the way he got all those kids to kowtow to us," Bobby said. "Now that *was* terrific. Without him, we'd never have gotten away."

Bobby and Dody threw the last of the chairs and carpeting into the disposal chamber. With the help of Elaine and Jonathan, they vacuumed the landing craft one last time, finally turning the vacuum hoses on themselves. The dust was gone; the bare metal of the lander's bulkhead was free of spores. Then they took turns in the lander's lone shower, waiting for the craft's meager water supply to be filtered and cleaned between each use. All of them, Hoffman included, tossed their dirty clothes into space and took fresh coveralls from the lander's cupboards.

The change of clothing transformed Hoffman. Washed and shaved, and trim in his clean space agency coveralls, he looked years younger, no more than Dody's age.

"I've been out of uniform for more than thirty years," he said, glancing at the one mirror aboard the landing craft. "It's a little strange, looking so respectable again."

They strapped themselves down to the bulkhead for landing.

Dody tried the radio once more. "Dead quiet," he said.

"I hope Mom and Dad are all right," said Elaine.

"Probably the receiver is just acting up," Dody said, not very convincingly.

"Dody," Hoffman said. "Go ahead and show us how you dock this landing craft. I'm ready to rejoin the fleet."

Actually Dody had very little to do, because Mickey the computer did most of the work, maneuvering the landing craft toward the open bay of the giant, rotating spaceship. "Reunion maneuvers begun," Mickey explained. The task was incredibly complex, Dody knew, but the computer handled it effortlessly and without incident.

"Prepare for docking," Mickey said sternly. He should have been programmed to say "please," Dody thought. If he were more polite, he might not seem quite so offensive.

The lander hovered in the launching bay for a few seconds while the doors slammed shut beneath them, and then the craft dropped down with a clunk.

"Hip, hip," said Bobby.

"Hurray!" answered Elaine. The color returned to her face. She was happy to be back to the *Wanderer*'s simulated gravity.

Mickey should have told them that they had landed safely and could now disembark, but he was silent. After checking the craft's instruments, the lander's crew descended into the bay.

It was empty and cold.

"I don't like this," Dody said.

"This is creepy," Bobby agreed.

"I hope Mom and Dad are okay," Elaine added.

Just then the inner doors opened. A small platoon of grown-ups in space agency uniforms rushed in, Sam and Betsy Ramsey among them.

"We've been so worried about you," said Betsy Ramsey as she attempted to hug all three of her children at the same time. Dody thought that they must look strange, all of them tangled together, a jumble of arms and heads and shoulders.

With tears slipping down her face, his mother said, "I wasn't sure we would ever see any of you ever again."

"Oh, Betsy," the captain said. "It was worrisome, I'll admit. But I always knew it would work out in the end." He embraced his offspring, one after another, giving Dody an especially hardy hug and roughing up his hair. "I finally got the crew awake," he said, gesturing toward the men and women who were busily inspecting the landing craft. "But Mickey clammed up on us. And we had a regular radio blackout. No communication at all. I couldn't send a crew down until we got everything fixed. And then we watched the entire planet wobble into a new orbit. The most damnable thing I ever saw. I was sure we'd lost you forever."

Sam Ramsey looked a little tearful, but he didn't cry. Instead, he became rather stern.

"Who was it," the captain asked, "who launched the lander to begin with? Was it you, Bobby?"

Bobby started to answer, but Dody interrupted him. "It was all my fault," Dody said.

"That procedure was outside your jurisdiction, Dody," the captain said, more mystified than angry. "You're lucky you weren't all killed."

"We had a sensational time," Bobby assured him.

"It was very scary, though," added Elaine.

"You can tell us all about it later," said Betsy Ramsey. "First you must introduce us to your friends."

"I'm Hoffman," the old man volunteered.

"You're not *the* Hoffman?" asked the captain.

"The same."

"But you aren't at all like your pictures," the captain noted.

"Who is?" Hoffman laughed. "The passage of time wears permanent paths across the face, like wagon ruts across the plains."

"It's an honor to meet you, sir," the captain said.

"The honor is entirely mine," said Hoffman with a courtly bow. It had been a long, long time since so many people had recognized just how important he once had been.

"And who's the young man?" asked Betsy Ramsey.

"That's Jonathan," Elaine said. "He's a very kind and courageous person. He wants to travel with us."

"Well, of course, he can. We can't very well leave him behind, can we?"

A wide grin opened up across Jonathan's face. His perfect teeth gleamed. Betsy Ramsey hugged the boy, as if he were one of her own.

"I'm *very* hungry," Bobby announced.

"I imagine you are," the captain said with a smile. He led them through the corridors of the *Wanderer* toward the dining hall — the mess, as he insisted on calling it. The Ramsey children noticed at once that the spaceship was alive with people and activity.

"The whole crew is awake now," the captain said. "I had to open up the hibernation valves by hand. Maybe that's when Mickey decided to stop talking and cut off all our radio communications. Once I got Charlie Madsen awake, the rest was easy. He's taken the entire computer system apart and is almost finished putting it back together again.

"We were getting ready for a rescue mission, but we would have been flying blind. We had no idea where you were, and Mickey wouldn't help us find you. Damnable computer!"

As they walked through the ship, Dody saw faces

he hadn't seen since they had blasted off from Earth together.

Some of the crew members whooped for joy at the sight of the Ramsey children. Quite a few hugged them. And still others applauded as if they were famous musicians walking on the stage to give a performance.

"Dody, is it you?" asked one woman who sat in the galley with a boy about Bobby's age and a girl a little younger than Elaine.

"What happened to Dody?" asked the boy.

Suddenly Dody recognized him. He was Billy Madsen.

"Billy?" he asked.

"That's right," the boy said.

"You look just the same," Dody said. "Just like you did before takeoff."

"*You* look a lot different," said Billy, who blushed to think that his remark might seem unkind. "I knew it was you," he said apologetically, "but you've changed a lot."

The girl sitting next to him was too shy to say a word, but Dody could see that she was greatly surprised. "You must be Anna," Dody said. For the first time in his life, he found himself talking to a child the way his own grandfather would. It was only a few decades ago when Anna had been one of his playmates.

"Hello, Dody," she said softly.

The Madsens left to make room for the newcomers. Before the portal closed behind them, Dody heard Billy say, "You told me Dody was going to be old, but not *that* old."

Silently the Ramseys and their guests dined on rehydrated chicken à la king again. "Never tasted better!" Hoffman exclaimed.

As they chewed and chewed and chewed on their chicken dinner, Bobby, Dody and Elaine told their stories of being chased and escaping, of finding Hoffman and recovering the landing craft, of Walter and his explosion in a puff of spores. Hoffman took a turn as well.

The Ramsey family was having a wonderful time, just as it did back on Earth when the father returned from a mission in space or the children came home from summer camp.

For the next several days, everywhere Dody looked, the spaceship *Wanderer* was teeming with scurrying crew members, like a nest of insects in his mother's vegetable garden. The full crew revitalized the spaceship, oiling all the moving parts, repairing the chinks and dents in its outer skin, and removing every possible glitch from the ship's computer. Mickey never looked or sounded lovelier. Not only did Billy Madsen's father give Mickey his voice back, but at Dody's suggestion, he even added the phrases "please" and "thank you" to the computer's working vocabulary. The change was intended to make Mickey seem more pleasant, but he didn't say the words as if he meant them. Dody thought that made him seem even more irritating than ever.

Finally Captain Ramsey reported to the entire crew that everything was ready for the long trip. It had always been the plan to return to Earth if their mission failed. "Let's go home, people," he announced over the ship's speaker system as he aimed the craft toward the distant star that was the sun. One pod of crew members after another went to its hibernation chamber to enter the long, deep slumber that would fill the journey back. Finally only the Ramsey family, along with Hoffman and Jonathan, were still awake, and now they, too, prepared for sleep, each one taking a long shower and putting on clean coveralls.

In the reddish glow of Hibernetics One, they bid each other farewell. Dody thought that he was the only one who felt the least bit worried about the long voyage that lay ahead.

"When we next wake up, we'll practically be back on Earth," Elaine said.

Hoffman looked pleased. "It's been a long time," he said.

"I can hardly wait to see it all," said Jonathan. "It must be so warm and wet."

Dody's feelings were so strong that he couldn't speak. It had been so very long since he had seen the planet of his birth. It couldn't possibly be as bright and perfect as it was in memory.

Each one embraced all the others, which meant a considerable amount of hugging before they were finished. They all found themselves saying things like "good-bye" and "farewell" and "godspeed," but they might have said "good night," because if all went well it would seem no more to any of them than a good night's sleep.

"Dody," said the captain, very sternly. "If you wake up before the rest of us, this time you be sure to wake up your mother and me. We've programmed Mickey to make that possible, you know."

"I will," said Dody. "I promise."

One by one they climbed into their berths and pulled the open sides closed around them. Jonathan slipped easily into his chamber, but Hoffman had considerable difficulty dragging up his legs and shutting himself in. "A bit like an old turkey trying to crawl back into its egg," he muttered to himself.

The last one into his perch, Dody found himself thinking about the planet Earth. It was blue and green and brown under a cover of swirling clouds. Most of it warm and wet. Jonathan would like it there, Dody thought.

He closed the latch and heard the hiss of gasses that would send him into the deepest kind of sleep. Warm and wet, he thought. The Earth as a whole was very warm and very wet.

The vapors numbed Dody's nose, and the numbness spread through his nostrils and mouth, down his throat and into his lungs, freezing whatever they touched on their way. He inhaled deeply and thought of his family's house in California and of the nearby beach where he liked to play on a warm day in the wet surf. The curling waves and the bubbly foam drove his rubber mattress high upon the shore until it squeaked against the sandy bottom. He thought of his mother and his father, trim in their swimming suits, sitting on a blanket under a broad umbrella. And there were his sister and brother, dripping wet, their slight bodies covered in towels and shivering as they sipped cold sodas that made them shiver all the more. Here, in the eye of memory, he, too, was young, a child of small dimensions and wiry composition. How nice it would be, he thought, to be a child again. To play at the beach that was at once both warm and wet, like the planet Earth itself.

The coldness spread out from his chest, into his arms and legs, up his neck and into his face, fanning out to touch his chin, his cheeks, his ears. At last, with his body still rising and falling in the surf of his imagination, Dody fell asleep.

When he woke up, he could not at first recognize the strange sound, the *chug-chug-chug* of the pumps removing the wake-up gases from his little chamber and replacing them with oxygen and nitrogen and a bit of carbon dioxide. He smacked his dry lips and felt extremely thirsty, and started to sit up in his berth. But then he remembered where he was and why it was that he was awake.

Dody had arranged for Mickey to wake him long before any of the others; he did the programming himself. The *Wanderer* had been on its way for only three months, covering only a fraction of the distance back to Earth. Dody had been asleep for ninety days, yet he found himself muttering, "I'm still so very tired," as he roused himself from his slumber. He turned the handle and opened the side of his chamber. His limbs felt a bit stiff as he slid out the narrow opening and jumped into the soft red glow of Hibernetics One.

He checked the berths below his own and was reassured to find his family in place, their sleeping profiles visible through the plastic bubbles. "You'll be OK," Dody assured them.

He limped about the room, his right leg still asleep and as numb as an artificial limb. He squatted down and stretched back up, and the exercise succeeded. He could feel the prickly return of circulation.

Moving more easily now, he soon found what he was looking for: another empty chamber.

"I'm not the only one awake," he reported to the sleeping forms. "I told you, Professor," he said, half expecting a reply from Hoffman's weathered face. But the old man, his profile visible through the plastic bubble of the scientist's berth, slept on. "You said that there was no need to worry, but I told you."

Dody was not sure where on the ship he would find the missing one, but there was no sense delaying the search any longer.

It was important to check every cabin and bay throughout the *Wanderer*, one by one if necessary. But he thought he knew where to begin.

In the control room, the dim running lights were on, and the large viewing screen was illuminated with stars against a pitch-black field.

"I thought I'd find you here, Jonathan," Dody said. "You've changed."

The boy was indeed transformed. Covered with a robe fashioned from a blanket, Jonathan's body was doubled over, with a great hump on his back almost equal in size to the rest of him. The face was unmistakably Jonathan's, but it was withered — not simply old but dried and puckered.

As Jonathan began to speak, a dusty cough came from his mouth. "There was nothing I could do," he said, his voice a throaty whisper. "I wish I knew how to make this stop."

"I wish that, too," Dody said. "But you're not one of us. Even the hibernation chemicals couldn't stop the sporing. You're 'the one among many,' aren't you? The one that Errat has chosen."

Jonathan spoke with difficulty. "We are still friends — aren't we? Even if this has happened."

Dody remembered the way Jonathan had thrown himself at the Winnems in his attempt to rescue Elaine. The way he'd led Dody to Hoffman and shown them the way back to the landing craft. The way he'd commanded the child's army to stop, just when the Ramseys were about to be beaten. He was brave and loyal. The Ramseys were lucky to have had such a friend.

"We'll always be friends," Dody said hoarsely. "Nothing can change that."

"I did so want to see the Earth you spoke of," Jonathan said. "The trees. The beaches. The mountains covered in snow."

"You would like it there," Dody said. "It's mostly warm and wet, you know. I wish that you could see it, but I know you wouldn't want to risk changing it forever."

Dody started to reach his hand out to the creature who had once been a boy.

"No, you mustn't touch me," Jonathan said.

Side by side, not touching, but close enough to feel the warmth of one another in the cool air of the spacecraft, they walked through the corridors.

"I know that I have to go," Jonathan said. The two had stopped in front of the ship's disposal bay.

Dody wanted to say that he was sorry, but he had lost the ability to speak. He tapped his code into the computerized lock and the door opened. The walls of the disposal bay gleamed like a newly scoured pan.

"Don't worry about me, Dody," Jonathan said as he shuffled into the chamber. "I'll find a home. Somewhere out there, on a distant planet of a distant star, a piece of me will spring to life again."

But *you* will be gone, Dody thought. The Jonathan I knew will be gone. Exploded into a cloud of spores, each particle a seed capable of generating a new Errat.

"I'll miss you," Dody said as he shut the door. He punched in the necessary signal to Mickey. "I really will miss you." A red light blinked above the doorway and with a great wheezing sound, the contents of the chamber were blown into the cold emptiness of space.

Dody walked about the spaceship for a while, hoping that he could shake off the gloom that hovered over him. He entered the solarium and lay flat on his stomach as the stars whirled by outside — a sight that always cheered him. But now he looked for a glimpse of his friend or the cloud of spores that his friend had become. There was no trace to be seen.

"I want to be home," Dody said aloud. "Right now."

He rose to his feet and found his way back to Hibernetics One. His open berth was waiting for him, and he climbed inside. He would sleep now, if all went as it was supposed to, for another century.

With the door shut, he closed his eyes and thought again of the long spit of sand washed by the waves of the Pacific. The escaping gases hissed, and the cold numbness spread through his body again.

Soon he would be home, he thought, but this time he'd be all grown up. And not just in body, but all of him. He was old now, too old for childish things.

But as he fell asleep he dreamed of the younger version of himself that would always be a part of him, no matter how old he became. And in his mind, he played again, with his friends Tony and Alan and with his brother and sister. And now, as distinctly as if he were there, he could hear the ocean roar on a distant and sandy shore.

A hundred years isn't so very long, he thought. It's no further away than morning.

About the Author

Paul Samuel Jacobs is a reporter for the *Los Angeles Times*. His first novel, *Born into Light,* began as a story for his three children and is now an SLJ Best Book. Mr. Jacobs lives near Sacramento, California, with his wife and family.

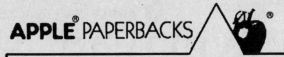